Praise for
NO STONES LEFT UNTURNED

"A masterfully crafted thriller, *No Stones Left Unturned* blends psychological depth, heart-pounding suspense, and a touch of the paranormal in a way that feels both gripping and real. Marie-Claude Gingras introduces readers to Leila Rose, a gifted yet grounded investigator who must navigate skepticism, danger, and her own abilities to uncover the truth. With vivid storytelling, richly drawn characters, and an intricate mystery that keeps unraveling until the final page, this novel not only captivates but also sets the stage for an exciting and thought-provoking series. A must-read for fans of crime fiction with a unique twist!"

—Jeffrey K Schmoll, author of
The Treasure of Tundavala Gap

"Imagine a Dana Scully with psychic powers. Imagine she's closing in on a dystopian, android-driven corporation that is literally more chilling than *WestWorld*. Now, add the misery of unsolved missing children cases. That's the powerful dynamic that drives this fast-moving futuristic thriller."

—Jeff Kramer, author of *Mud Season*

"Marie-Claude Gingras' scientific background adds credibility to her depiction of Leila Rose's telepathic skills. Leila works with FBI partners in tracking kidnapped children from Vermont to Alaska, unmasking political chicanery, corporate thievery, and murder."

—Ray Collins, author of
Setup and *The General's Briefcase*

"This compelling thriller follows Leila, a brave, warm-hearted psychic, as she searches for missing children and uncovers unsettling secrets along the way. With a mix of suspense, action, and a touch of sci-fi, the story keeps you turning pages while highlighting courage, resilience, and the power of human connection. A great read for those who enjoy fast-paced mysteries with heart."

—Aniko Sabo, PhD, computational biologist

"Caught in lengthy flight delays and missed connections resulting in long hours of waiting in a boring airport? Immerse yourself in the lecture of *No Stones Left Unturned* as I did, a fast suspense thriller that keeps you at the edge of your seat. But readers, beware, you will be so captivated by the story that you could miss your rescheduled flight and forget to eat a bite before getting on the next plane!"

—Eugene Roussel, PhD, biotech CEO

"*No Stones Left Unturned* entices a reader to continue on, page after page. Just when you think you have it figured out, a plot twist. To anticipate what may happen and to leave a reader stunned makes them crave more. Foreshadowing of what may become of humanoids and AI in our daily lives intrigues the reader as our world continues to take steps towards that reality along with the controversies of having a sixth sense in today's society. The epitome of a suspenseful story of a parent's worst nightmare that leads to something greater than what was expected."

—Monica C. Sulit, reader

"Marie-Claude Gingras has an undeniable talent as a writer! Her first thriller is excellent; it keeps us in suspense. I really appreciated the original angle brought by the character of Leila, the expert with special gifts. Enjoy reading!"

—Marie Godbout, reader

"In *No Stones Left Unturned*, author Dr. Marie-Claude Gingras creates a gripping mystery full of action, twists and turns, and surprises. The dialogue gives an enchanting old-world feel to the story, which contrasts nicely to the futuristic setting. When Leila encounters new experiences that threaten her comfortable life, she finds allies with myriad skills to guide and protect her as she seeks to solve the mysterious abduction of children. Her willingness to help the families is not only informed by but also enhanced by her telepathy. The integration of very ancient technology and very futuristic technology creates another contrast similar to the use of language in dialogue that intrigues the reader. The plot is unique and draws the reader in, particularly with how each section begins, engaging the reader. It was a very fast read, and I was left with many questions about the interpersonal interactions between Leila and Ryan that will hopefully be answered in future books."

—Dr. Gloria Fawcett, reader

No Stones Left Unturned
by Marie-Claude Gingras

© Copyright 2025 Marie-Claude Gingras

ISBN 979-8-88824-634-4

All rights reserved. No part of this publication may be reproduced, stored in a retrieval system, or transmitted in any form or by any means—electronic, mechanical, photocopy, recording, or any other—except for brief quotations in printed reviews, without the prior written permission of the author.

This is a work of fiction. All the characters in this book are fictitious, and any resemblance to actual persons, living or dead, is purely coincidental. The names, incidents, dialogue, and opinions expressed are products of the author's imagination and are not to be construed as real.

Edited by Becky Hilliker
Cover design by Catherine Herold

Published by

3705 Shore Drive
Virginia Beach, VA 23455
800-435-4811
www.koehlerbooks.com

NO STONES LEFT UNTURNED

MARIE-CLAUDE GINGRAS

VIRGINIA BEACH
CAPE CHARLES

To Eugène, the companion of my life's journey.

Contrary to our belief, our destiny is not entirely under our control. Whatever the path we set our eyes on, whatever our determination to follow it, events can trigger mechanisms that forever change our existence.

PART ONE

CHAPTER 1

Martha and Jeff's Farm

Vermont, July 7, 2036

MARTHA WAS RACING back home. She didn't feel the weeds lacerating her legs; she barely noticed where she was stepping. Thoughts were scrambled in her head; she could not control them. Scenarios flashed in her mind, but none made sense, and none were acceptable.

As she approached home, she saw Jeff on his way back in the distance. He was alone on his tractor, confirming her worst fear. A tornado of despair ripped her heart apart into a thousand pieces. She could not breathe anymore and fell on her knees. Covering her face with her hands, she emitted a guttural, wrenching scream—the sound of a wounded animal.

It took her several minutes to find the courage to get up. Wiping her hand across her eyes, she gulped back her tears and began running again. She had to reach home—and Jeff.

The morning had been overcast, but after lunch, the sun had timidly pierced through the clouds, promising a lovely summer afternoon. As she put away the last lunch dishes, it was as if a draft of wind had gone through the kitchen, and the screen door of the family's old farmhouse slammed shut. She turned just in time to see her nine-year-old son, Stephan, joyfully running toward the pond with his fishing gear and his dog, Charlie, a boisterous golden retriever. Once again, she proudly imagined the two inseparable friends featured in a picturesque Norman Rockwell painting. They were such a lovely pair. She smiled. Her love for her exuberant little boy with his endless imagination was even more profound than her love for Jeff, her soulmate and husband.

"Don't forget, Stephan, no swimming before your father gets there," she called from the back door before he got out of ear shot.

Stephan was not allowed to swim alone, even though he was a natural swimmer, and not even if he was with Charlie, who would surely intervene if he got in trouble. But to Stephan's delight, Jeff had mentioned at lunch that he might join him for a dip after completing his tasks on the farm.

"Sure, Mom," Stephan answered, waiving back at her before taking the path that led to the pond. He knew better than to disobey, as the punishment for disobedience was the confiscation of his most prized possession—his fishing gear.

By late afternoon, Stephan and Charlie had yet to return home; Martha thought Jeff had cut through the fields to get to the pond, so she decided to join them. The footpath to the pond was lined by wildflowers, creating a vibrant tapestry. As a painter, she got lost in the beauty of the scenery for a moment. A song came to her mind, and she started singing. Distracted, she did not notice the oddity at first: no sound of frolicking came from the pond—no laughter, no splashing, no barking—just utter quiet.

The path opened. The song died in her mouth. The pond and the little pier were deserted. Stephan and Charlie were nowhere to be seen, and neither was Jeff. Puzzled, she wondered if perhaps Jeff was teaching Stephan about nature somewhere close by.

She walked up to the end of the pier, where she could get a broader view of the pond. There, she found the fishing rod lying on the boards, a worm now dried out, still hooked. A sense of foreboding washed over her: Stephan would never carelessly abandon his precious fishing gear to wander around, even with Jeff.

She hesitated, listening for sounds. Then, she frantically called out several times. The only answers to her calls were a bird chirping and her heart pounding in her ears.

Where were they? Why was Jeff or Stephan not answering? At least Charlie should have barked back. Something was wrong, horribly wrong. Stephan would not have ventured far from the farm without asking for permission. Jeff would have stopped by the house to let her know if they would have gone elsewhere. He knew better than to leave her unaware. Her worry was now turning into a gripping panic.

She desperately searched the surroundings to find evidence indicating where they might have gone. She found none, no footprints at the water's edge, no sign of trampled weeds or broken reeds.

And suddenly, reality hit her like a lightning bolt. Memories of distressed and anguished friends and neighbors surfaced in her mind. She had never imagined this could happen to her family, to Stephan. He had been on their property, so close to their house. It couldn't be.

Beside herself, she raced toward the house.

CHAPTER 2

Mrs. Rubinstein

Houston, July 8

IT WAS APPROACHING midnight when Leila's cell phone rang. She was stretched out relaxing in her living room, listening to a harp concerto by François-Adrien Boïeldieu. Her voice-activated phone graciously informed her that Mrs. Evelyn Rubinstein, one of her clients, was calling.

It had been a long day: several clients, questions, advice, shows of compassion. Leila wanted, needed time to unwind and clear her mind, so she didn't answer. A few seconds later, her phone rang again, only to stop and start again and again in what seemed to be a relentless and endless dance. What could warrant disturbing her at this time of night? She finally resigned herself to answering Mrs. Rubinstein's fifth call.

Mrs. Rubinstein looked visibly upset on the phone screen. She had no makeup on, her hair was disheveled, and worry lines creased her face. The thirty-five-year-old usually projected a perfectly manicured, well-dressed, and confident presence. Leila had never seen her in such a state.

"Ms. Rose, I'm so relieved to finally reach you," she said before

Leila could voice a word. "I must talk to you; it's a matter of life or death."

"What is it about?" Leila asked hesitantly, unsure what to think. Mrs. Rubinstein was a drama queen who quickly blew up small events out of proportion, so Leila doubted that whatever she was agitated about was truly worth disturbing her so late.

"I will stop by your place to explain," Mrs. Rubinstein answered, hanging up before Leila could agree, leaving her perplexed as she stared at her phone's dark screen.

Mrs. Rubinstein reached Leila's home in record time, rang the bell, and then frantically pounded on the door. As Leila opened the door, Mrs. Rubinstein pushed past her in a fury and entered the living room. She sat on the edge of the sofa and immediately began to spew forth her story.

"Ms. Rose, I am so sorry to disturb you at this late hour, but time is running out. Yesterday, Stephan, my nine-year-old nephew, went fishing with his dog and never returned home. Both have just vanished without leaving any trace."

She then continued hastily, "You must help us. I've already booked you a seat on a plane that leaves in a few hours. You will arrive in Burlington early in the afternoon."

"What—"

"My sister Martha will pick you up at the airport. She will stand by you and stop anyone from interfering with your work, including family and friends. Emotions in the community are running high right now, and unfortunately, the opposition to your presence is strong."

"Who—"

"My brother-in-law Jeff has a medieval perception of you. For him, you are the equivalent of a witch, a counterfeiter. He has appealed to one of his college fraternity friends in Washington, DC, who is now a member of an FBI elite tactical team specializing in rescue missions for abduction cases and hostage situations. Three members of his team are already on-site with him. They are action people; they don't believe your extrasensory perception gifts can help. More accurately, they don't believe in the existence of such gifts."

Then, reluctantly, she said, "On the other end, the police chief is against external intervention of any type. He believes that if Stephan has been abducted, the kidnapper will continue to hide him, and all this pandemonium won't lead anywhere and might even obscure any clues."

Mrs. Rubinstein finally paused. Leila's head was spinning. She had picked up Mrs. Rubinstein's call not even an hour ago; over the last few minutes, she had been informed of a child's probable abduction, a flight booked without her consent, solid opposition to her presence, and of doubt about her capacity to solve the case.

As Mrs. Rubinstein was about to speak again, Leila raised her hand and the woman fell silent. She knew Mrs. Rubinstein wanted to add that she was convinced she alone could find Stephan, and his life depended on her, but Leila did not want to hear it. She needed a few minutes to dissipate her tension and emotions. She closed her eyes and took a few deep breaths, hoping to regain control.

Opposite thoughts collided in her head. It would be a daunting challenge of a magnitude she had never faced before, and a failure would have dire emotional consequences. Still, her refusal would also result in emotional turmoil if the child was never found. The possibility that her intervention could have resulted in a happier ending would haunt her forever.

Mrs. Rubinstein took Leila's hands in hers. Leila opened her eyes and saw a mixture of desperation and hope in the other woman's eyes.

A tear rolled down Mrs. Rubinstein's cheek. More than anything she could have said, that single tear broke Leila's resistance.

Leila realized that whatever would happen and the resulting consequences, only one option would ultimately allow her to be at peace. She hugged Mrs. Rubinstein and, in a firm voice, said, "I will do everything in my power to find your nephew."

A shadow of a smile formed on Mrs. Rubinstein's lips as she murmured, "Thank you."

Over the next hour, Mrs. Rubinstein informed Leila that the kidnapping had taken place at the pond on the family farm located near Springtown, a small town—more of a village—in Windsor County, Vermont, a region where beautiful and vast wooded areas surround farmlands. She described it as a close-knit community where everyone knew each other, as most residents had been born and raised there.

But what she added next surprised Leila. "Unexpectedly, for such a place, several boys and girls between ten and thirteen years of age have disappeared from the county in recent years. My nephew is the youngest."

The children's disappearances didn't reflect any exclusive sexual attraction: the gender was not a constant and the age range was broad, exhibiting no consistency usually associated with such predators. The thought triggered an alarm in Leila's head and acid in her stomach. Could there be a sex trafficking ring in the area? She didn't voice the question out loud, not wanting to frighten Mrs. Rubinstein further.

Until now, Leila had found her work as a personal life consultant fulfilling. She even believed she was destined for this job. At her birth thirty years before, her father had named her *Leila*, which means "night" in Arabic. He had chosen the name for its symbolism when associated with her last name, Rose. He believed his child would become a loving soul standing out in the darkest time, a "rose of the night," bringing hope for a better future.

Her name, the extrasensory perception gifts and telepathic skills inherited from her mother, the education she received from her parents, and the empathy she had acquired had shaped her life to advise and guide others in their struggles.

But unknown to her, the tragic event happening miles away was about to turn her simple and eventless life upside down and connect her with those who would reorient her future and give her life a whole new meaning.

CHAPTER 3

Unexpected Welcome

Vermont, July 9

During the wee hours of the night, Mrs. Rubinstein informed her sister of Leila's arrival and conveyed the information Leila had requested. Unknown to Martha, Jeff called her back to express his concerns for his wife, who had not slept or eaten in the last thirty hours. They decided that Leila would first remedy Martha's exhaustion before she collapsed.

As Leila exited the airport security zone, a young woman with dark circles under her eyes, curly blond hair tied into a ponytail, and wearing a beige dress accentuating her pale skin walked toward her. Her physical fatigue was so significant that it was apparent she could barely stand up. She was drawing upon whatever energy she had left from her love for her child.

"Madam Rose, I'm Martha. I can't tell you how much I appreciate your help. My sister Evelyn has spoken so highly of you. I'm convinced that you will find our Stephan."

"Nice to meet you, Martha. I surely hope I can help," Leila sincerely answered.

"Tell me what you need, and I will do everything I can to

accommodate you."

Looking at Martha intently, Leila felt a vast mental emptiness in her. She no longer had the wherewithal to interact with her surroundings.

"Martha, *you* are my connection to Stephan. I need you, but you cannot help in your current state of exhaustion. We'll delay the road trip to your farm and get a room at a nearby hotel, where you will rest until tomorrow morning."

"That's impossible," she rebelled. "I can't sleep. I'm worried sick. I cannot bear the thought of losing my Stephan forever. Moreover, time is of the essence—every minute counts."

"I can only find Stephan through you; I'll help you relax. Did you bring the information I requested? I'll educate myself while you rest. We'll not lose any time. Tomorrow, we'll discuss everything during the two-hour drive home."

Given Leila's adamant attitude, Martha no longer resisted. After settling in the hotel room, Leila gave her what she needed for the night, courtesy of her sister. She did not seem surprised, her extreme fatigue preventing her from reasoning and questioning anything. Acting on Leila's recommendation, she took a long hot bath. She then sat on one of the queen beds and handed Leila a large envelope she had retrieved from her purse.

"This contains a map of the region, the list of its inhabitants, how far they live from our farm, some of their personal information, where the other children who have disappeared lived, and the press releases about their disappearances."

Leila's surprise must have been apparent. Martha smiled shyly and added, "Jeff has a digital version that he gave to his friend, but he believes you are at least a hundred years old, with no modern aptitude, so he made you a printed copy."

Leila smiled back at her. "It's always fascinating to see how people associate perception gifts with withdrawal from modern society," she concluded as she removed the stack of papers from the envelope.

"Let me show you our location on the map," Martha started but never elaborated further as Leila mentally conveyed that everything was under control and that she could rest. Her body relaxed, and she lay down without further opposition. She was asleep in less than two minutes.

Leila quietly left the room and went down to the hotel lobby. It was a perfect location for her intended work without disturbing Martha. First, she wanted to copy the information on her laptop, then get Jeff's opinion about his neighbors and friends and add his comments and her perceived impressions beside each name.

There were very few people in the lobby other than hotel employees. It consisted of a large atrium with sitting areas where guests could relax. It was surrounded by shops, business glass offices, and a restaurant with a terrace facing the atrium. Leila chose to sit in a comfortable armchair with a soothing view of a miniature garden in an outside enclosure. She took a moment to admire the garden's perfect shape and vibrant array of colors.

For a reason she could not explain, she felt highly nervous. The view didn't calm her as it otherwise would have. She pushed her uneasiness aside and juggled the numerous papers and her laptop. Unused to such simultaneous handling, somehow, she made an unfortunate movement. Before she could catch them, all the documents on her lap fell on the marble floor, some sliding out of her immediate reach. So, she slipped out of her chair and knelt, leaning to reach the farthest paper.

As she went through the motion, she heard a hiss over her head, followed by cracking glass. She looked up and saw a bullet-sized hole and star-shaped cracks in the glass panel where she'd had an unobstructed view of the garden a few minutes earlier. Puzzled, she looked back at the armchair. It now had a hole right at the height where her head had previously been. She froze in denial. How could that be possible? Was someone trying to kill her?

If not for Jeff's misconception of her technological aptitudes and her clumsiness, a perfect crime would have been committed. The assailant must have used a silencer, because no shot had rung out. Her fate would not have been discovered immediately since she was not in anyone's direct view. Only a blood pool on the marble floor would have finally attracted attention long after her death.

Adrenaline surging, and without another thought, she quickly rose and looked around her, hoping to locate her attempted killer. The shot had come from inside the lobby, but no one was there. Her assailant had already left. She had taken too long to react. She raced to the front desk.

"Did you notice someone in the lobby a minute or two ago?" she asked the clerk.

The young man smiled politely and calmly answered, "I did not see anyone other than you, but I would be happy to convey a message to any of our guests if you wish."

A surge of frustration and anger rose in Leila. She wanted to yell back that this was not a courtesy call, that she almost had been killed in the hotel lobby under his complacent watch, and that he needed to react accordingly. However, looking at the clerk more closely, she realized he was a humanoid, an artificial intelligence robot programmed to handle simple requests.

So Leila returned to sit in an armchair, this time facing the atrium. The adrenaline rush was over, and she started to shake. She took several deep breaths to calm herself down enough to think of the appropriate next course of action.

Should she call the police to report the attack? No one could corroborate her story. The holes in the armchair and window might have been there for days, if not months. Would the police believe she could be the target of a shooter? She was not from the region, and no one knew her here. Could she even reveal the reasons she was here? Her experience told her that, more than anything, it would be assumed she was a nut job and the event would be disregarded.

The attack indicated that her killer knew who she was, why she was here, and how and when she would arrive. Then, realizing they were not going to Martha's farm, he must have followed them to the hotel. Now that his first attempt had failed, what would he do next? Would he try again later today or tomorrow or even cause a deadly accident on their way to the farm?

She decided to talk to Jeff before doing anything next.

Jeff answered her video call quickly, expecting her to reassure him of Martha's condition as requested. The dark circles under his eyes told Leila he was not in much better shape than his wife.

She didn't give him time to say a word and immediately asked him, "Jeff, who, outside you and Martha, knew I was coming today?"

"Ms. Rose, why are you asking me this? What's going on?" he asked worriedly, discerning the distress in her voice.

"I am in the hotel lobby. Someone just tried to kill me."

Leila immediately saw by his facial expression that he doubted her sanity. His exasperating answer corroborated her impression.

"You surely are making a mistake. The fatigue of the journey must be affecting your perception," he said in a soothing voice as if addressing an anxious child, someone having a breakdown, or a mentally challenged person.

Leila took a deep breath to hold her temper in check before answering, "Jeff, I am thirty years old; I can withstand a short plane trip quite well. Further, the hole a bullet makes in the back of an armchair and a window previously intact leaves no doubt."

As she talked, she moved her phone camera over the starry hole in the window so he could see it. He frowned and looked perplexed.

"Let me talk to my friend. He works for the FBI. He'll know what to do. I'll call you back in a few minutes," he said.

Less than ten minutes later, Leila's phone rang. Despite the call originating from Jeff's cell phone, it was not him but a very handsome man with piercing deep-blue eyes contrasting with his rich mahogany hair and facial features reflecting a hard-core strength of character.

"Good afternoon, ma'am. I'm Ryan Steele, Jeff's friend. Can you tell me exactly what happened? Have you alerted the authorities?"

Leila related the events and concluded, "I have not notified the police yet since I wasn't sure what would be gained by it."

"You did well, ma'am. Stay calm, in plain sight of the hotel staff, and be alert, but don't worry. I don't think the killer will try twice at the same location, especially now that you know his intent. Robert Cassidy, one of our criminal branch regional agents, should be there shortly. He will text you upon arrival but will ignore you in public. He'll put together the best plan for your safe return to Houston tomorrow. Please give me your room number. Do you have any questions?"

Yes, she did have at least two major questions and a comment: Why did he assume she would leave tomorrow? If so, why did he think she wouldn't have a say in any plan being formed? His arrogant, macho demeanor was infuriating. It was not for him to decide what she could, should, and would do. Once again, she took a deep breath. Now was not the time to question his behavior and commanding know-it-all attitude. She swallowed her pride and politely answered, "No. I have no questions," and she gave him her room number.

She soon received a text announcing Robert's arrival. A tall, athletically built Black man approached the reception desk and booked the room adjacent to hers. She preceded him to the elevator. He followed her in but ignored her. They unlocked the connecting doors a few minutes after entering their respective rooms. She stepped into his room, and they correctly introduced themselves. They spent the late afternoon and early evening planning for the next day. Unlike Ryan, Robert didn't take for granted that she would follow his order and did not address her condescendingly. Even under the current circumstances, he was a pleasant, calm, and respectful human being.

CHAPTER 4

Rigged Exit

July 10

MARTHA WOKE UP around seven the following day as breakfast was delivered to the room. She stretched, remarking to Leila how the eighteen hours of sleep had done her a world of good. She even dug into the fresh fruits, cereal, jam, eggs, toast, and muffins with gusto.

They left the room within the next hour. Robert joined them in the elevator and acknowledged their presence with a brief, impersonal nod. As the elevator reached the lobby, he hurried out.

Several people were now strolling in the lobby or finishing breakfast at the adjacent restaurant. Once again, Leila perceived a malicious feeling directed toward her. She shuddered. She stopped abruptly and turned toward Martha, who was still unaware of the preceding day's assault.

"Martha, I am sorry, but due to events outside my control, I must return to Houston immediately," Leila told her.

The announcement completely threw Martha off, and she burst out crying.

"Please, don't. You *must* find Stephan. I put all my hopes in you."

"Martha, please don't cry. Your husband has put together a good team, one of the best. They'll find Stephan. Trust them."

"How can you abandon us? Jeff was right; you're nothing but a quack," she snapped.

Contrary to what Martha thought, leaving her in this state broke Leila's heart. She was also worried about Martha's safety, but Robert had assured her Martha would be protected by agents already in place.

The airport shuttle had just arrived, and Robert and other customers were boarding. Before getting in the shuttle, Leila glanced back. Martha was still where she had left her, her face streaming with tears, hoping Leila would change her mind at the last minute.

The door of the shuttle shut behind Leila. She no longer felt Martha's despair or the threatening gaze of her assailant. As the shuttle pulled away, she let out a sigh of relief.

From the airport security lineup to the boarding area, Leila had a stronger-than-ever nagging sense of anxiety. Her would-be attacker must have shadowed her, but the crowd was too dense to identify him. She discreetly nodded to Robert to let him know what she suspected. He looked around but was unable to pinpoint any suspect.

Leila boarded the plane and quickly took a place in the first-class section. She watched the other passengers slowly stroll past her down the aisle, perceiving no aggressive feelings toward her. Once everyone had finally taken their seats, the flight attendant discreetly looked at her and nodded, closing the curtain between first class and coach. Leila hurriedly got up, grabbed her carry-on suitcase the flight attendant had kept in the first-class service kitchen, and stepped out into the gangway. The flight attendant closed and securely locked the plane door behind her, preventing anyone from following her.

Leila walked up to the door giving access to the boarding area and waited fifteen minutes for the plane to take off and for an agent to open the door to the terminal. As she reentered, she didn't perceive any threat; her attacker was gone. She hurried toward the drop-off area and got into a car parked immediately in front of the entrance.

"All went as planned?" Robert asked.

"Yes. Everyone played their roles perfectly. I didn't feel threatened when I stepped back into the terminal. How's Martha?"

"Much better. When you left, one of our agents took her to an office and explained what was happening. She drove to our rendezvous point and is now waiting for us. No one else, outside one of our agents, followed her."

"I hope she'll forgive me for hiding the truth from her. She reacted exactly as we had hoped and made my retreat quite believable. It must have convinced my assailant of the uselessness of killing me. He just followed me to make sure I was boarding the plane."

"Don't forget; our plan was designed to thwart the bad guys and ward off any danger to Martha. Unfortunately, success will be short-lived. The future doesn't bode well. Your assailant probably fears that you could identify him. A threatened and cornered beast will attack, and the bulletproof vest you are now wearing under your clothes won't protect you against everything. It's not too late to board the next plane for Houston."

Leila sensed that Robert had more than her survival in mind; he was annoyed. She couldn't resist asking him, "Ryan is angry that you didn't force me to leave. Isn't he?"

A faint smile appeared on his lips.

"Denying it would be useless—he's furious. He's very concerned he'll have to shift part of his workforce from finding Stephan to protecting you. And there's more: a few years ago, the family of a lost girl pressured him to work with a self-proclaimed clairvoyant.

It didn't end well. The false leads and delays it caused resulted in the child's death. Ryan has never forgiven himself for that. He swore he would never listen again to, and I quote, 'any other mentally disturbed charlatan.' He'll give you a hard time," Robert explained.

"The mere ignorance of what I can do is at the origin of his opposition to my presence and the source of my assailant's fear. I'm not a psychic, and I cannot predict the future. I can read people's minds and learn about their life experiences to better understand them. I perceive their feelings, love bonds, the thoughts connecting people, and the distress signals they send to one another. Through these vibrations, I can establish contact and visualize surroundings and locations. I could be miles away from the action. In this case, I only need Martha to connect with Stephan."

The rendezvous point was a private airfield. Martha stood near a small plane talking to the pilot, a bulky man in his mid-forties. She came to Leila, visibly concerned about how she had addressed her in the hotel lobby.

"Madam Rose, I am so—"

"Martha, please don't. I should be the one apologizing. We were counting on your outburst to convince the killer I was leaving. Moreover, please do me a favor: call me Leila. The Madam attribute gives me the impression of being one of those fortune tellers and crystal ball and palm readers often seen in old movies. And this will reinforce Jeff's misconception about me."

Martha smiled at the analogy, visibly relieved Leila wasn't holding a grudge against her. They walked toward the pilot after thanking and saying goodbye to Robert.

"Leila, let me introduce you to Joe Graham. Joe oversees a branch of our operations, transporting fresh products from our farms to our upper-end customers in the city. Jeff has tasked him to bring us back home safely."

"I'm glad to help," Joe said, visibly upset by Stephan's kidnapping. "I hope you can end this nightmare and find Stephan. He's a sweet boy."

Joe took his role very seriously. He flew several times over the region. Leila, who had never been to Vermont before, was amazed to see how beautiful it was. Green was the dominant color, with fields alternating with forests and hills with valleys. Small villages were interspersed among those, and here and there, reminiscent of old times, covered bridges dotted small rivers and streams. Martha added details as they flew over her house and the pond where Stephan had last been seen. Upon landing, they found Martha's car beside Joe's plane hangar. She had programmed it to drive there automatically upon arriving at the rendezvous point. They headed home without delay.

CHAPTER 5

Search Operation Command Center

July 10

THE COMMAND CENTER for the search operation had been set up in Martha and Jeff's living room. Giant screens, computers, a massive table, and chairs had replaced the usual furniture, which had been pushed into a corner. Real-time visual and infrared thermal footage of the surrounding woods was being transmitted by drones and displayed side by side on the screens. A grid map covering the vast perimeter was color-coded, indicating the areas already searched and those up next. Five men were checking the different footage. Leila recognized Jeff and his friend Ryan among them.

Leila's bedroom was on the second floor, so she tiptoed behind Martha toward the adjacent stairs. She wanted to avoid drawing attention to her presence, hoping the men would be too absorbed by their task to notice her. Unfortunately, Jeff heard them and, like a magnet, was drawn to Martha. Following Jeff visually, Ryan saw Leila in the background. Before Jeff or Martha could react, Ryan made a beeline toward her. In a second, all the pent-up frustrations of his previous failed rescue mission and the emotional stress associated with the present unsolved one merged to create a level of anger that boiled over and spewed at her like a sudden volcanic eruption.

"You shouldn't be here, lady. Don't you understand the seriousness of your situation? We can't babysit you. We have a child to rescue," Ryan said vehemently.

"Thank you for your concern, Mr. Steele. Your compassion touches me," Leila said, sustaining his look and losing her temper, confronted by his arrogance and unjustified aggression. "Don't mind me; I'll stay out of your way."

His eyes narrowed, and his look grew more intense, but a knock sounded at the front door before he could respond. For a moment, no one moved, as they were surprised and caught in the scene's intensity. Then Jeff went to answer the door, grabbing Ryan's arm and squeezing it slightly on his way there, a silent plea to calm down.

"Walters, come on in," they heard Jeff say.

A man in a sheriff's uniform entered the house. Looking around, he hesitated momentarily, perceiving the odd atmosphere. He turned back to Jeff, then said, walking toward the screen displaying the grid map, "I came to tell you that the folks have organized another search for later today. Let me show you where it'll be."

Ryan said to Leila through his teeth, "Do us all a favor and go home before it's too late." He turned around to join Jeff and the sheriff. The men all regrouped in front of the color-coded map.

Leila took Martha aside. She needed to get away from the oppressive atmosphere that was still lingering around her.

"Let's walk up to the pond," she said.

"I want to apologize for Ryan's behavior. I've never seen him act like that. I don't understand what got into him. He's usually such a nice guy."

"Don't worry. I know better than to be affected by the bad temper of an ill-mannered man."

However, Leila couldn't help but wonder if the constant contact with Jeff and especially Ryan would permanently affect her calm, affectionate, and trusting personality: she had found herself bursting out in anger or having to restrain herself so many times in the last twenty-four hours.

The pond was serene and quiet, the reeds trembling under the light wind the only audible sound. Martha and Leila walked to the pier and sat down crossed-legged, facing each other.

"You love this place, don't you?" Leila asked, feeling the peaceful, soothing vibrations of nature surrounding them.

"Yes, we come here often in the evening. It can be very romantic when the moon is full, and the frogs are singing their love," Martha answered, radiating happiness for a brief moment.

"Martha, I want you to hold on to this feeling of happiness. Think about all the occasions when you were with Jeff and Stephan, simply enjoying life together," Leila said.

Martha stared into the water. Leila took her hands in hers. She visualized a stream of cherished memories: Jeff imitating Stephan carrying back home his dream catch, Big Mouth, a four-foot-long imaginary trout, a trout almost as long as he was tall; Stephan playfully splashing cold water at Jeff from a stream where they had stopped to rest during an excursion in the woods looking for mushrooms, and Jeff reciprocating, both soon drenched and laughing their heads off. And so many others.

Suddenly, through Martha, Leila connected with Stephan, responding to his mother's love thoughts. He was alive. He was not hurt. He was with Charlie and watched over by a funny-looking robot about his size, offering him food and playing with him. Stephan was not afraid. He quite liked his new companion, but he missed his parents. He wanted to return home, play outside, and be with them.

Through his mind, Leila saw that the room he was presently in was large and without windows, with concrete-reinforced walls painted in a light pastel-purple color. It was furnished with a bed, a small table, two chairs, a cushioned loveseat, a large screen hooked on a wall, and a few lamps, all in concordant colors. A paravent most likely hid the bathroom facilities in one of the corners. On the far wall, a small refrigerator and a microwave could be seen under a row of cupboards. Even though confining, the space was comfortable and cheerful. It did not smell musty. However, nothing could help identify its location or owner.

Leila snipped off her mental connection with Stephan.

"Stephan is alive and not injured. He is being held in a place watched over by a funny-looking robot," she told Martha and then described what she had seen.

Tears of joy silently rolled down Martha's cheeks. "Thank God. It is not too late. However, I have no idea what and where this place could be," she said.

"We should ask some old folks. This might have been built decades ago," Leila suggested, hopeful.

"Willie, Joe's father. He might be able to help us. He has been around a lot and knows so much about anything and everything. I will contact him and find out when he can meet with us while you unpack."

They walked back home at a fast pace, the hope for a happy ending giving Martha a burst of energy.

Leila's room was bright. An old-style white iron bed was covered with a floral bedspread and matching cushions of different colors. Nightstand tables on each side of the bed, a massive dresser, and an antique vanity set with a mirror completed the decor.

Leila was admiring two paintings of a garden signed by Martha hung on the wall above the bed when Jeff knocked at the bedroom door she had left open and walked in. He looked determined. Leila instantly knew the reason he was here. Martha had told him she had established contact with Stephan and had described what she had seen.

"Ms. Rose, my back is against the wall. I want Martha to remain as positive as possible through this ordeal, but I don't want you to fill her head with information that could well turn out to be false. It will make it harder for her to face the truth when the time comes."

Before Leila could answer him, she saw Martha standing in the doorway, her face flushed and her hands clenched.

"I choose hope over despair, Jeff. This is my way of coping with the situation. We have talked about this before. We had agreed to respect each other's choice of action for finding our son. Don't interfere now," she told him defiantly.

"Martha, please—"

"Get out. I don't want to argue with you."

Jeff looked at her, about to answer, but changed his mind and left the room, his head down, more worried than angry. Martha took a moment to regain control of herself.

"Sorry about that. Well, by now, you know where everyone stands. On a more positive note, Willie will see us anytime now."

The road leading to the town was scenic: forest-covered hills, cute red barns, horses running freely in a large field, and, to Leila's delight, a covered wooden bridge. Springtown had been settled in this picturesque pastoral setting at a bend of the meandering river in a verdant valley. Old houses, white picket fences, and a little church on a hill dominating the parish were part of its charm.

The two-story assisted living facility had been recently built, but its architecture did not offend the eyes, respecting the town's old-world signature. A well-dressed man in his early seventies awaited them at its entrance. He was leaning on a nicely chiseled cane in a very gentlemanly posture. He greeted them warmly, and for a moment, Leila thought he would kiss her hand. He was so charming.

He took them to the back of the building, where they sat under a gazebo surrounded by a lovely flower garden. The air was saturated with the perfume of nearby rosebushes that dominated the floral arrangements. It was a perfect harmony of bright and subdued colors. Leila recognized the garden Martha had used as a model for her paintings.

"This is a wonderful garden," Leila told him. "It's your creation, isn't it?"

He looked at her and smiled softly.

"Young lady, the town has been buzzing about you. There might be truth in what I heard you can do. I sincerely hope so. How can I help?"

She described what she had seen and asked him if he knew of any such place.

"With climate change, tornadoes around here have become more frequent and stronger. Many folks have built a safe room in their basement, but nothing like what you are describing. This sounds more like a doomsday shelter."

"A doomsday shelter?" Martha said, astonished.

"Yes, a bunker that can withstand radiation in a nuclear war. During the Cold War with Russia, many people believed that someday some idiot would press the button and end our existence. Everyone wanted to build one for a while, but I'm unaware anyone has done so here. However, I have a small army of old folks here who will happily investigate. I'll let you know as soon as I find anything."

They said their goodbyes. As they left, Leila looked back at him. He was already down to business on his phone, contacting his soldiers.

"He is a good man," Martha said. "Everyone loves him, especially kids. Occasionally, the school invites him to narrate a historical event and guide the kids to reenact it. The kids then present a representation of the play they have worked on to their parents and the town."

Martha's judgment of the man reflected Leila's thoughts. He would go out of his way to help them.

"Now, what should we do?" Martha asked.

"Contact as many people as you can. A mass inquiry should pressure the kidnapper to react."

"Won't this be dangerous for Stephan?"

"I don't think so. I think instead I will once again be his target."

CHAPTER 6

The Assisted Living Facility

July 11

LEILA WOKE UP in the middle of the night with a sickening feeling and a sense of urgency. She dressed quickly and went downstairs. The house was quiet. The master bedroom door was closed. She could hear Martha's and Jeff's unsynchronized regular breathing. She cursed herself. Ironically, she should have been more "clairvoyant" and gotten Willie's cell phone number. She telepathically called Martha's name several times and asked her to join her. A minute or two elapsed, and she heard her getting out of bed. Martha finally opened the door with a puzzled and concerned look. Leila did not give her time to reflect on what had just happened and dragged her to the kitchen.

"Willie's life is in danger. Please, call him."

Martha didn't question her, trusting what Leila said. She dialed Willie's number several times without success.

"He is not answering," Martha said worriedly. "I'm calling the facility emergency number. There is always a nurse on duty. If she is not in her office, the call will be relayed to her cell phone."

"Keep trying. Meanwhile, please instruct your car to drive me there," Leila told her.

"*You* are not going *anywhere*," Ryan thundered behind them.

They both jumped, startled. Neither of them had heard him coming. Leila turned to him, furious.

"I won't sit here while a man is being murdered. Go back to bed, wherever that is, put in some earplugs, and be oblivious to what's happening around you."

"This is strange—the nurse isn't picking up either," Martha said, puzzled, momentarily interrupting Leila and Ryan's tense exchange.

Ryan looked at Martha, slightly annoyed.

"It can be for a lot of good reasons." Then, looking at Leila, he added sharply, "Lady, I will drive you there and prove your *perceptions* are wrong—just an overactive imagination or inconsequent nightmare. Then, I will personally lock you up in your room, where you will stay out of my sight for the remainder of the night."

"Fine, but if I am right, you will show me some respect and call me by my appropriate name, even if it burns your tongue. Let's go; there's no time to waste with stupid arguments."

Ryan picked up his phone, and surprised, Leila heard him say, "Pick up the night shift; I have to go out for a while."

Leila felt a rush of guilt. He had not been asleep; he was guarding the house. Was he doing so because of a possible threat to her? Was he feeling responsible for her safety, or did he think her presence put others in the house in danger? She promised to uncover the real reason when they got back.

Ryan meant it when he said he would drive her there. His car was old, and Leila suspected it had no autopilot. Pictures from the vintage movie *Back to the Future* flashed in her head. In any other circumstances, she would have paused to consider the silly thought that this macho man was a time traveler from the last century, car included, and would have burst out laughing. But she was presently scared to death. Ryan's driving was more appropriate on a racetrack than on a country road, where he had to dodge potholes and nocturnal animals adventuring on the road. She was happy it was dark; he couldn't see the fear on her face.

They reached the village in a fraction of the time it would have taken with a car on autopilot. Leila directed him to the assisted living facility. They were stunned and speechless as soon as it came into view. Flames were leaping out of the windows of the right-corner apartment on the second floor. There was no fire alarm or siren to be heard. No one was running around or yelling—no policemen, no firemen, no residents. All were unaware of the danger; all were asleep.

Leila jumped out of the car before it had fully stopped. She heard Ryan swear. He called after her to wait for him, but it didn't slow her down a bit. The adrenaline rush had her moving at a run as she headed across the concrete parking lot toward the front door. He raced behind her, simultaneously calling 911. They both arrived at the front door together. Surprisingly, it was unlocked. No one was at the reception desk.

"Hello," Leila yelled.

No answer.

They walked toward the offices. Seeing a fire alarm, Ryan pulled it, but nothing happened. Leila could see puzzlement reflecting on his face. Someone must have rendered it inoperative. One door labeled *Infirmary* was ajar. Ryan pushed it open. The nurse and the janitor had their heads in their arms, slumped on the desk.

Ryan checked their vital signs.

"They are alive but drugged. They are safe here for the moment. We must first take care of those threatened by the fire."

He took the nurse's access key card and gave her the janitor's keys.

"You should be able to enter everywhere with these keys. A

facility like this should have an intercom in one of the main offices. It will put you in communication with all the apartments. Alert the residents of the fire and tell them to evacuate immediately. I'll see if I can save the occupants of the burning apartment and those next to it."

"Based on what Martha told us, Willie's apartment is number 210. It is also located on the second floor but faces the garden. Please check that he is unhurt," Leila implored.

"I will," he answered.

He hesitated a moment and handed her his gun. Leila looked at him, stunned.

"Leila, something evil is happening here. Whoever orchestrated this might still be around. Don't let anyone get close to you. Use the gun if necessary."

And he was gone. Leila stood frozen for a moment; not only did he trust her with his gun, but for the first time, he had called her by her name, and his attitude had been neither belligerent nor arrogant. He was sincerely concerned. She felt momentarily relieved and hopeful: their future interactions might not always be on a battlefield.

She found the intercom control panel in the second office she checked. She informed the residents that a fire had been detected in a second-floor right-wing apartment and ordered them to proceed as they had been taught during the fire drill. She assured them the firefighters would soon be here to help those in need. She repeated the message several times in a pressing but reassuring voice.

Ryan reached the second floor and ran toward the apartment on fire at the end of the corridor. An intense heat radiated from the door, indicating that the fire had reached the front of the apartment.

Opening the door would be disastrous: the air from the hallway would rush inside the apartment, and the oxygen would fuel the fire. Smoke was already filtering through the door frame. It was too late; he could not help the occupants. He had to save the residents of the surrounding apartments.

He then heard Leila's calm but firm voice broadcast everywhere. He had to admit she was level-headed as well as strong-minded. Doors opened, and people started to get out.

Ryan asked one of the residents, a man who seemed to be in better shape than the others, to direct everyone toward the central stairs. "You know your neighbors. Please make sure that they are evacuating. I need to check apartment 210."

The man nodded and pointed at a closed door farther down. "Right there."

Using the nurse's key card, Ryan accessed Willie's apartment. A smell that he did not immediately recognize hit his nostrils. He went straight to the bedroom, where a man was lying across the bed in an awkward position. As Ryan approached the bed, he distinctly heard a click. The head of the bed instantly ignited. Ryan lifted the man in his arms and ran toward the door. Looking back, he saw the fire spreading to the mattress and the adjacent furniture.

His mind registered three facts. First, the fire had been initiated by a timed device. Second, the fire was propagating too fast. The smell. His mind connected the dots: a fire accelerant. Third, the bedroom sprinklers should have been triggered by the fire. Crossing the living room, he looked up at the ceiling. The sprinklers had been covered and hermetically sealed with heavy-duty plastic bags. He assumed the bedroom sprinklers had suffered the same fate. A similar setting must have been used in the other apartment consumed by the fire.

Ryan hated to admit it, but Leila had been right; Willie's life was in danger. A few more minutes and it would have been too late. Willie must have learned something that would compromise

Stephan's kidnapper, a clue worth killing him and at least one other resident for.

Ryan emerged out of the residence carrying Willie in his arms. For a moment, Leila thought Willie was dead. But when she saw Ryan refuse a fireman's help and go straight to one of the ambulances brought in, she understood that Willie was alive and that Ryan had taken him under his watch. She joined them.

"Ms. Rose here will be riding with the patient in the ambulance," Ryan told the medics with authority, stopping them from closing the back doors.

Then, looking at her, he added, "From now on, Willie shouldn't be left without one of us close by. I'll follow the ambulance and join you at the hospital."

CHAPTER 7

Nurse Brody

July 11

LIKE THE NURSE and the janitor, Willie had been drugged, but he was unhurt. Ryan's intervention had been perfectly timed. Ralph, the resident of the corner apartment, had not been as lucky and had died in the fire. The coroner was performing his autopsy to determine whether he had also been drugged.

The doctor released Willie from the hospital shortly after the sheriff interviewed him. Joe and his wife wanted him to live with them, but Ryan vetoed the idea. Finally, it was decided that Willie would move into Martha's and Jeff's house until further notice. The sheriff was unhappy about this arrangement but could not argue against it for a fundamental security reason: Willie would live among highly trained professionals qualified to protect him against any eventuality.

Leila, Ryan, and Willie arrived at the house around eleven in the morning; everyone was in the living room, waiting patiently for them.

"Willie, meet my team," Ryan said. To Leila's surprise, turning toward her, he added, "Leila, please forgive my rudeness. I failed to introduce you to my team yesterday."

He went on, indicating a flamboyant, bony man in an orange T-shirt that matched his red hair but contrasted with his white skin. "This is Alex, our expert informatician." Then, pointing to the two other contrasting muscular men, he added, "Jack and Pete, field agents. They have all volunteered to help find Stephan."

Leila was still processing Ryan's 360-degree change in attitude when Alex gave her an enthusiastic handshake and Jack and Pete offered a more reserved nod. Willie, whose life had most likely been uneventful until recently, was visibly impressed and excited to meet these men of action. The events of the last eighteen hours had rejuvenated him. He walked with a more confident step, and there was a spark in his eyes. At Ryan's invitation, he recounted the preceding day's events for the team.

"After you left yesterday afternoon," Willie said, looking at Martha and Leila, "I called several residents and scheduled an emergency meeting for seven thirty that evening. We were at least fifteen to brainstorm without success for about an hour. We concluded that our best chance to identify the bunker owner and its location was to talk to Ralph, who was sick and couldn't attend the meeting."

"Why Ralph?" Leila inquired.

"He worked as a day laborer all his life, doing any job for whoever had a need. There isn't a single household in this community he didn't work for."

"So, you all believe he might have built or helped build the bunker?" Leila asked.

"Without a doubt. Now that he is gone, God bless his soul, it will be hard to know who owns the bunker, where it's located, and to identify Stephan's kidnapper."

"Was your meeting behind closed doors?" Ryan asked.

"Oh no. We were in the facility lounge."

"So, everyone passing by could hear you? It's then possible that the kidnapper, a.k.a. the arsonist, a.k.a. the killer, is a resident of this town," Ryan explained.

"I would even go so far as to say he or she works or lives at the assisted living facility," Alex added.

All heads turned toward him.

He added, "I hacked into the security system last night before the sheriff confiscated the recording and downloaded the entire night's recording from every point of entry. Besides the staff and residents, no one else entered the facility after Martha and Leila left."

"At what time does the personnel night shift start?" Ryan asked.

"At seven. It's a twelve-hour shift."

"So, whoever committed these crimes heard your discussion and planned Ralph's murder and the fire after the night shift started," Ryan commented.

"The only in-and-out movement last night was from the nurse. She went out for a few minutes."

"Let's view it."

They regrouped before the giant screen and saw the nurse talking on her cell phone near a back entrance. Surprisingly, she did not make eye contact with her interlocutor but surveyed her surroundings. She then went to what might have been her car. As she reached it, she dropped her purse, lowered herself to retrieve it, and, in the process, disappeared from the camera field. After several minutes, she stood up and returned to the facility.

"Why take her purse outside just to talk on the phone?" Leila wondered.

"Why did it take her so long to pick up her purse?" Pete asked.

"Its contents must have spilled out on the ground. She had to pick up everything," Jack hypothesized. "If she is like my wife, her purse contains her entire life."

"Odd—she went to presumably her car but didn't get in. Why?" Ryan said. "Alex, can you replay the recording in slow motion?"

As they were watching again, Martha got closer to the screen.

"The contents of her purse could not spill out. I have an identical purse; the zipper tab has an ornament attached. It's visible here, see? The tab was in the closed position the entire time."

"Well, I'll be damned. Something did happen by the car, but we couldn't see it," Ryan exclaimed. "A small robot probably carried the fire accelerant and the two devices to start the fires. The parked cars hid the robot from the surveillance camera. The nurse intentionally dropped her purse, allowing her to retrieve the items without raising suspicion. She had easy access to sleeping pills at the infirmary and heavy-duty plastic bags to cover the ceiling sprinklers in the kitchen. *Et voilà.*"

"Oh!" Willie exclaimed. "She came to see me for gardening advice as I went to bed. She apologized for the late hour but said she had been too busy to come earlier. She offered me a delicious herbal tea she had made with her garden flowers and plants, and we both drank it as I answered her questions. She left soon after, and I barely made it to my bed. I was so sleepy."

"She must have spiked your tea and done the same with Ralph," Ryan concluded. "She returned after you were both asleep to set up the fire devices, timing each with a different delay. Then, she went downstairs, offered the drugged tea to the janitor, and drank it herself to make us believe she was also a victim."

"I will find her address," said Alex.

"The sheriff made it clear that we have no authority to do anything and strongly recommended that we stay out of his line of work. So, Pete, Jack, let's go see him and tell him what we have learned. Then, we will pay the lady a visit whether he likes it or not. He can come with us or stay behind."

Once again, Leila couldn't help but notice how pejoratively Ryan was using the *lady* attribute. She was pleased to be no longer associated with Ryan's list of unworthy citizens.

CHAPTER 8

Stephan

July 11

RYAN, PETE, AND Jack had gone into town, Jeff and Alex were discussing how to research the bunker owner, and Martha was showing Willie his new living quarters, so Leila decided to walk up on a little hill near the house where a weeping willow stood alone, creating an oasis of calm and natural beauty. From there, the view extended to the horizon. She could see the pond, the fields, and the line of trees at the edge of Jeff's property. She sat in the natural enclosure formed by the roots and the trunk.

Closing her eyes, she became oblivious to her surroundings, and her mind drifted away. She found herself in a forest, facing a stream. The air was filled with the music of the water flowing between green mossy rocks soft to the touch. The light was dim, filtered by the tree foliage. It was a beautiful area. Visually following the water flow at countercurrent, she saw a rock formation from which the stream surfaced from its underground source. She did not know where she was, but seeing Charlie lying at her feet, she understood. She was visualizing where Stephan was presently through his mind. She probed his memory to learn how he had reached this place, but there was a gap between when he fell asleep the night before in the bunker and when he had awakened here a few minutes earlier.

Leila cut off her mental connection with Stephan and sprinted to the house. She was out of breath when she burst into the living room. Her entrance did not go unnoticed by the four occupants of the room, who wondered what was happening. Raising her index finger, she asked for a minute to compose herself.

"Have any of you ever seen this place?" she asked, describing the stream and its surroundings without mentioning Stephan's presence.

"Yes, I have," answered Willie. "It's called the Enchanted Spring. It's at the origin of a legend in which a young girl—"

"Forgive me for interrupting you, Willie, but is it far from here?" Leila asked.

"It's about an hour's drive by back roads and then at least another hour's hike through the woods," he said, visibly surprised by her impatience and disappointed by her lack of interest in his story.

Leila turned toward Martha and Jeff.

"That's where Stephan is presently. You told him once that he should stay near a water source if lost in a forest. Someone brought him there, and he is waiting for you to find him."

"Yesterday, you said he was in a bunker. Now, he is in the woods! You expect us to believe you each time you daydream and change your mind!" Jeff said, incredulous and exasperated.

"One does not exclude the other," Leila snapped impatiently.

Willie raised his hand to stop Jeff from answering and said softly, "If I were you, I'd seriously consider what Leila is saying for two reasons. First, she was right about the bunker. Ralph paid for its knowledge with his life, and I almost lost mine. Second, how can she know about the Enchanted Spring? She's not from around here, and the site is certainly not advertised as a tourist attraction."

Martha took Jeff's hand and pleaded, "I can go there with Willie if you want to pursue your search of the bunker with Alex. We can bring a drone and confirm Stephan's location before venturing into the forest."

"Take Unhide," Alex suggested. "It has a heat sensor. But Jeff, why don't you go with them? I can manage by myself. No stone should be left unturned."

Leila looked at Jeff, sensing he was conflicted about what to do. Even if his attitude exasperated her, she empathized with him.

"How did you get these recordings?" Sheriff Walters roared.

"That's not the point, Sheriff. The fact is that no one else but the facility's nurse had the opportunity to set up the fires. You need to pick her up and question her if we want to know who is responsible for Stephan's kidnapping and find him," Ryan answered in a matching tone.

"How about I arrest you instead for obstruction of justice."

"Fine by me. And I will do everything in my power to ensure everyone knows how you bungled this case and, instead of arresting the murder suspect, you arrested a witness."

"You are in no way a witness and have no authority here. Moreover, you hacked into the surveillance network of a private facility. You might even have altered the video recording you just showed me. And now you're threatening me. That's it. I'm placing you under arrest."

A young man fulfilling administrative duties hesitantly raised his hand before saying, "Sheriff, I can confirm the video's authenticity. I saw the same footage on the original recording we confiscated from the facility."

The sheriff looked at him, visibly upset by the interruption. Consequently, he was losing face and momentum. For a moment, he remained silent, deciding what to do next and the consequence of doing nothing; then, he barked his orders to the young man.

"Contact Edward. He is on patrol. Tell him to stop by Nurse Brody's house. We'll join him there." Then, looking at Ryan he said, "Follow my car. Don't even think of rushing to get there before I do."

It took longer than usual to get to the house, the sheriff intentionally giving Ryan and his teammates a tour of the town at a languid pace. When they finally reached it, they saw Officer Edward standing on the other side of the street, talking with a young woman who was gently swaying a young baby in her arms. Officer Edward joined them as they exited their respective cars.

"Well, Sheriff, I was talking to Angelica, Nurse Brody's neighbor and a cousin of mine. Poor Angie, her baby keeps her up almost every night. She walks him around the house to calm him down. She is exhausted."

"Edward, come to the point," said the sheriff impatiently.

"Well, at around six this morning, she saw Nurse Brody putting suitcases in her car and driving off in a hurry."

"We should get in the house to see if we can find anything incriminating," said Ryan.

"Hold on, mister. We respect the law here; we cannot storm the place without a search warrant from the county judge," announced the sheriff in a simulated offended tone, hiding his satisfaction at putting Ryan back in his place.

"Well, Sheriff, since Nurse Brody is renting this place from your wife, as the owner, she can authorize us to get inside and check if everything is fine. It would be a lot faster," suggested Officer Edward.

Strike two, Ryan thought as he watched the sheriff's face turn red and his eyes bulge out in anger.

Willie helped Jeff navigate the back roads. When he told him to stop at an isolated location without specific visible landmarks,

Leila wondered.

"Willie, how could you know this is the right spot?" she asked him.

"A friend brought me here for the first time over fifty-five years ago. He showed me the distinctive landmarks to follow to pinpoint this place."

"You came here only once?" Leila said, impressed.

He looked at her with a smirk.

"No, I came a few times by myself to make sure I would recognize the place. Then I told the legend of the Enchanted Spring to a few girls I wanted to impress and brought them there. A mystery always fascinates and can help gain some favors. I was young back then and relied on artifice to conquer."

He winked at her and burst out laughing.

"I'm ready," said Jeff, who had stepped out of the car to set up Unhide and ensure the data would be transmitted to his laptop. "We should be able to detect the spring's location based on its lower temperature."

"The spring is straight west from here, through the forest. You then follow the water flow at countercurrent to reach the Enchanted Spring location that Leila visualized," said Willie.

All eyes were glued to the screen as Jeff maneuvered the drone above the tree foliage. As expected, he found the spring and set up the drone's speed to allow the heat sensor to detect any living organism. Thirty minutes, an eternity, elapsed before a four-legged creature appeared on the screen. Jeff turned the camera on and slowly lowered the drone between the trees.

"It's Charlie. Oh my god, it's Charlie!" Martha screamed.

"Stephan should be a bit further down," Leila said. "There he is!"

Stephan had heard the drone and was waving at it. Charlie was jumping and barking. Martha burst out crying. Leila took control of the drone from Jeff's shaking hands. Jeff wrapped his arms around Martha as much to comfort himself as his wife. He looked at Leila and whispered, "Thank you."

A few minutes later, Martha and Jeff left to get Stephan, who was following the drone back. Leila saw Willie wiping away a few tears as they entered the forest. Even at his advanced age, he was still handsome, and she could easily imagine how he must have broken several hearts when young.

She smiled and told him, "For what it's worth, Willie, as a young girl, I might have followed you there too. You have at least an hour to convince me before they return with Stephan. Tell me the tale of the Enchanted Spring."

CHAPTER 9

Celebration

July 12

THE HOUSE WAS effervescent with joy. Martha and Jeff had invited everyone to celebrate Stephan's safe return. The word that he had been found unharmed and that Leila had been instrumental in resolving the kidnapping had spread like wildfire. She had become a celebrity overnight, and everyone wanted to take a selfie with her. To escape the buzz, she took refuge under the weeping willow. Barely twenty minutes had passed when she heard the muffled sound of footsteps on the grass.

"Everyone is wondering what happened to you. Tired of being in the spotlight?" Ryan said jokingly.

"Yes. Contrary to what you might think, I don't like to be the center of attention; I'm uncomfortable in this role. You can take my place in the sun if you want. You and your team should also be credited for your actions."

"We also prefer anonymity."

They were silent for a moment. To an outsider, they seemed to just be enjoying the tranquility of the site, but for Leila, it was evident that they were both tortured by a persistent thought that spoiled their happiness of having rescued Stephan. She concluded that one of them had to confront their feelings openly, so she said, "Ryan, can I be honest with you?"

"Of course, but for once, I might know what you're going to tell me. We might have rescued a child but haven't solved the other sporadic abductions. In a few months or a year or two, another child will be abducted, then another. We suspect that Brody is an accomplice and murderer, but there is still an unidentified mastermind pulling the strings behind the scenes. You, like me, are not at peace with leaving this place."

"Exactly. You read my mind!" she said, looking at him teasingly. Then, she added more seriously, "Can we solve this by working together? Would you be willing to bury the hatchet for good?"

"Leila, I apologize for my previous attitude. Preconceived ideas overtook me. Yes, we should work closely together. It can save innocent lives."

He smiled, suddenly aware of the irony of his statement, considering that a few days ago, he'd wanted to get rid of her even before being introduced. His view of her "skills" had shifted from skepticism and denial to consideration and trust.

"I made a list of involved individuals and questions related to each. If we find the answers to any of these, we'll come closer to identifying the mastermind behind Stephan's abduction and Ralph's murder," she said as she handed him a folded paper she was carrying with her as a constant reminder.

Using the flashlight of his cell phone, he read it.

—*Leila*: *Who knew I was coming here, is a fine shooter, and was out of town the day I flew in and part of the following day?*

—*Nurse Brody*: *Who contacted and sent her what she needed to set up the fires? Where is she now?*

—*Ralph*: *Who owns the bunker he helped build? Where is it located?*

—*Willie*: *Why kill him? What does he know that threatened*

Stephan's abductor?

"One definite person of interest should be added to your list," said Ryan. "Sheriff Walters. Why was he so reluctant to collaborate with us? After all, he was seriously understaffed for such an operation. Why did he want to stop us from interacting with the nurse and janitor at all costs? Why did he want to arrest me instead of investigating the possible role of the nurse in the fires? And finally, where is he now?"

"Are you thinking he can be the operation's mastermind?" Leila asked.

"He also sure knows how to use a gun and could be your attacker. It will be necessary to determine where he was the day you flew in, but one thing is certain: he was not there the night of the fire; I only saw Officer Edward."

"So that evening, he could have supplied Nurse Brody with what she needed to start the fire, driven to the woods to drop Stephan, and then been there the next morning to interrogate Willie."

"Yes. In addition, Nurse Brody was renting the house she occupied from his wife."

"You're right; this is very compelling. Officer Edward is here tonight. I will take advantage of my newly acquired fame and use some of my charms to learn more about Sheriff Walters without raising his suspicion," Leila said as she unbuttoned her shirt a bit lower.

"And in the meantime, I will take advantage of Willie's admiration of men of action to ask him a few questions," he said, following her lead and unbuttoning his shirt, bringing his muscular chest with well-defined abs into plain view.

"I am not sure this display of muscles will work as well with Willie," she said, unwillingly admiring his sculpted torso.

"Let's see which one of us gets the most out of it."

They both looked at each other and burst out laughing, a laugh lightened by the alleviated tension between them and the happiness of having reached a mutual understanding.

Officer Edward had been celebrating a little bit too much already. He was not inebriated but in a trusting mood. He was delighted to get the attention of the guest of honor when Leila approached him, all smiling and flirtatious.

"Officer, I don't think we had the chance to meet personally," Leila told him.

"Well, please, call me Edward."

"Please return the favor by calling me Leila. I admire the work you and Sheriff Walters are doing here. The crime rate is so low surely due to your vigilance."

"Well, it's a good community, so we can't complain. We've had only one single murderer in the whole history of the village, Nurse Brody, and she isn't one of us; she is an outsider. I think that, with her gone, the kidnappings will also stop. In any case, Sheriff Walters and I will stay on top of it," he said, inflating his torso and stretching his arms over his head.

"I am sure people will feel safe now," Leila said, letting her eyes linger over his torso, which unfortunately could not sustain any comparison to Ryan's. She chastised herself for the thought and added, "By the way, I haven't seen Sheriff Walters tonight. I hope he's not sick. This is such a happy occasion and a good party. I'm sad he's missing it."

"Well, Beth, his wife, requested that he take some time off so they could celebrate their wedding anniversary."

"Ah, wedding anniversaries are so important. I hope they went to some exotic place."

"Well, Ms. Rose, hmm, Leila, people here aren't used to going to fancy places by the sea. We love our wilderness. I'm pretty sure they went to Beth's grandfather's house. It's about thirty minutes from here, but it's pretty isolated. The old man didn't like company and ensured no self-invited person would set foot on his property without impunity."

"Have you ever been there?"

"Well, I've never been invited. I don't think many people have been either. The old man cared for Beth after her mother died there giving birth to her. He never even sent her to school. She turned out a bit wild like him. It's no surprise she didn't want to be here tonight. She hasn't attended any village celebrations since the accident."

"An accident? A car accident? Did she end up with some physical wounds or scars and doesn't want people to see them or something?"

"Well, not exactly. About ten years ago, the village had a New Year's celebration. Everyone was there, even those with sick kids at home. These folks assumed they were not contagious and that it was fine for them to come to celebrate. Doc said they must have carried the disease and transmitted it to Beth, who had never been vaccinated for any diseases. Beth was pregnant at that time. She blamed the good people of the village when she miscarried due to illness. Not only did she lose her child, but she remained infertile."

"Oh, gosh. What a tragedy."

"Well, everyone apologized. But I don't think Beth ever forgave them. She wasn't quite the same after that. A few months after the miscarriage, she was admitted to a fancy out-of-state center that treats emotional distress. Since then, she has been going there at least once a year. Sheriff Walters says that it keeps her balanced. She comes back almost normal—for a short time, at least."

Ryan joined them at that moment. "I am sorry to interrupt. Martha is requesting you, Leila."

Leila said goodbye to Edward and followed Ryan.

"I fulfilled my part of our agreement; I found Walters. Were you able to talk with Willie?" she asked him mockingly. His shirt was buttoned up again, and she knew he hadn't been able to do so, having seen him being stopped several times on his way by several well-intentioned women.

"You were right; displaying my attributes was a bad idea. I underestimated the strong attraction I exert on women!" he said jokingly.

Leila rolled her eyes and burst out laughing. Then, she told him what she had learned from Edward.

After Martha's thank you speech and toast, they finally approached Willie.

"Willie, I was wondering if you had thought about why Nurse Brody wanted to kill you. It's still not clear to me," Ryan asked, a puzzled expression on his face.

"I understand. It's bothering me too. I came up with only two reasons: the belief that Ralph had told me who owned the bunker or that I knew where Stephan would be dumped."

"Or because you knew the people who knew the Enchanted Spring," Leila added pensively.

"What? You lost me here."

"The spring isn't easy to find. You told us some landmarks helped locate it. But at night, those might be hard to see. Only someone who knows the place well would find it in the dark. Who, outside yourselves, would know how to go there?"

"They are all dead or have left town—the guy who told me about it, the girls I brought there."

"What about Sheriff Walters," Ryan inquired.

"Yeah, now that you mention it, he might know about the place. The guy who brought me there and told me about the legend was his uncle."

Leila felt Ryan's heartbeat drastically increase.

"Oh, by the way, Willie, speaking of Sheriff Walters—we want to say goodbye to him before leaving tomorrow. But he isn't here and is unreachable by phone. Officer Edward told me earlier tonight that he and his wife were most likely celebrating their wedding anniversary at Beth's grandfather's house, a secluded place that only a few people have ever visited. Would you be, by any chance, one of them?"

"Yes, I've been there long ago, but my knowledge of the place is limited. Beth didn't sell it after the old man died; growing up there, she must be attached to it."

They would have continued in this line of inquiry but were interrupted by Joe, who was coming to get Willie.

Willie explained, "With Stephan found, Nurse Brody on the run, and you guys leaving, I am relocating to Joe's house, where I will stay until I can move back into my renovated apartment."

Then, looking at Ryan, he said, "Once again, thank you for saving my life."

Winking at Leila, he added, "I wish I could be forty years younger, Leila. I would have enchanted you."

She laughed and hugged him. "It was a real pleasure to know you, Willie. Take good care."

After the last guest left, they gathered in the tidy living room. The search equipment was gone, and it had transformed into a cozy place inciting discussion and exchange. Stephan had gone to bed, and Martha and Jeff were radiating happiness. Alex, Pete, and Jack were in a light mood, laughing and joking. Leila's and Ryan's reserved attitudes contrasted with those of the others.

Looking at them, Jeff asked, "What the hell is wrong with you two? You have such gloomy faces. Are you sad to leave us? Please know that you're welcome back here anytime."

"I have an idea," Martha said. "How about we mark this date as the official date for an annual reunion to celebrate Stephan's rescue?"

"That's a nice thought, Martha. I'm sure we would all love to come back here to celebrate," Leila said. Then, looking at Ryan, who nodded, she added, "Meanwhile, I think we owe you an explanation for our sad disposition." She then shared their hypotheses and impressions about what they had learned that evening.

As she concluded, Ryan added, "I have serious doubt about Sheriff Walters's integrity. I'm inclined to believe he might be Leila's shooter, Stephan's kidnapper, and the mastermind behind Ralph's murder. I also believe the bunker is at Beth's old man's house. Based on what I heard, it would likely agree with his personality. We should pay him a visit—and the sooner, the better."

"From what I know about that place, you should not go there at night. Moreover, you might encounter some resistance to getting a search warrant without solid proof. Our judge is Walters's cousin," Jeff concluded.

"Ah, those close-knit places where people are all related one way or another to each other. However, I'm confident that I can overcome this obstacle. I'll make some calls tonight, and by tomorrow morning, we should be set for an unofficial impromptu goodbye visit," Ryan replied confidently.

CHAPTER 10

The Old Man's House

July 13

THE FOLLOWING DAY, a very unhappy and slightly hungover Officer Edward joined them about one mile from Beth's old man's house. Following Edward's instruction on the land layout, Alex flew Unhide over the property.

"I can't detect anyone's presence, but there is for sure a bunker adjacent to the basement," he said, pointing to an opaque, impenetrable rectangle space protruding underground from the right side of the house.

"This visit has now become an official inquiry," said Ryan.

"Well, this doesn't mean anything. There might still be more than one bunker in the region. I don't believe Sheriff Walters is the man you described. He will never forgive me for bringing you here," Edward complained.

"Stop whining, Edward; you had no say in what's happening. I'll make sure Walters understands it. Let's go," Ryan ordered. Turning toward Leila and Alex, he added, "Be on your guard. If Walters is really what we suspect, he is dangerous, a person not to mess with."

"Not to worry, I'll be ready," said Alex, pointing at the gun beside him.

"Be careful, Ryan. There must be a reason why everyone is so scared of the place," Leila said.

"We'll take all necessary precautions," Ryan assured her.

They transferred their equipment into Edward's police car, and Edward drove up to the house driveway. Alex and Leila were at the forefront of the action, following its live development thanks to the drone broadcast. They saw Pete, Jack, and Ryan geared up and walking the distance between the road, the outbuildings, and the house, their assault rifles ready to fire. They looked impressive, and Leila understood who these men were for the first time. Edward followed them, unprotected, his weapon in its holster; he had refused to follow Ryan's advice.

The men scouted around the house and entered the sizable independent garage. Alex switched the broadcast from the drone to those of the cameras and communications devices Pete, Jack, and Ryan were equipped with. A car and an SUV were parked in the garage.

"Wait, this is Nurse Brody's car. What's going on here?" Edward exclaimed, wide-eyed.

"He must be shocked," Leila muttered to Alex. "That's the first time I've ever heard that guy start a sentence with anything other than "Well.""

Alex smirked as he raised the volume on the drone's broadcast.

"The SUV?" Pete asked Edwards.

"Sheriff Walters's," Edwards verified.

"Let's go inside the house," Ryan said intensely.

Edward revised his position and pulled out his weapon. He now looked nervous. The four men surrounded the house, each accessing it through a different point of entry. After searching every room and confirming that no one was there, they gathered in front of the basement door. Ryan went down first, followed by Edward, then by Pete and Jack.

Broken furniture, boxes, and a jumble of objects were barely discernible in the basement's scarce light. Such clutter made it a dangerous place. They fanned out in different directions, maintaining contact between them and Alex.

"Gotcha," Ryan said. I found the bunker's entrance. A stack of boxes blocks its access. Jack, come and help me move them aside."

Jack joined Ryan to clear up the space. A heavy metal door with a wheel came into view. They examined it, ensuring it was not connected to any explosive device. Reassured, they slowly turned the wheel. The door opened, and in the dim light filtering through the basement, Alex and Leila saw what looked like two bodies lying on the floor. At this exact moment, they heard a distinct click from Pete's communications device and heard him yelling, "Edward, don't move."

But it was too late. A flash of light filled up the section of the screen displaying the live feed from Pete's camera as the noise of an explosion could be heard. Leila and Alex saw Ryan and Jack being hurtled inside the bunker and heard the door close behind them under the explosion's impact. All transmissions went blank.

"No," Leila yelled, distraught by the implication of what they had just witnessed.

Alex frantically switched Unhide's transmission mode. An infrared view of the basement appeared. A fire was raging in one of its corners. Nobody could be detected due to the heat generated by the fire. However, the fire was not propagating, and they assumed the basement was equipped with sprinklers. They watched as the fire decreased in intensity until it was finally extinguished.

"I must go see what can be done to help them," Alex said, and looking at Leila perplexed, he added, "It's against protocol to bring a civilian to the site of a disaster. But I cannot leave you here either. It might not be safe."

"Let's go; I don't give a damn about your protocol. Remember, none of you have any official authority here. You volunteered."

"It's not exactly true. That's only what the sheriff would like to believe."

"You really want to have this discussion right now?" Leila said, exasperated.

"Oh, hell and damnation, you're right. Let's go."

As they approached, they saw Jack and Ryan exiting the house. Ryan had his arm around Jack's shoulders, and Jack, with his arm around Ryan's waist, was supporting him. Their clothes were soiled and soaked in blood. Leila jumped out of the van and ran toward them. Holding his hand up, Ryan stopped her from getting closer.

"It's not safe. Neither of you should be here."

His breathing was short, he was holding his side, and he was visibly in pain. Leila suspected that he must have several broken ribs.

Seeing the worried look on Leila's face, Ryan added, "It's okay. Don't worry. We were thrown to the bunker floor by the force of the explosion, and my assault rifle hit my chest. My vest absorbed only part of the impact."

"Where is Pete?" Alex interrupted.

Jack shook his head. "Edward must have stepped on an explosive device. Pete was close by. Neither made it," he said with an altered voice, visibly shaken by the loss of his teammate and friend.

Alex looked away, but not before Leila could see his eyes filling with tears. She could feel his intense sadness and rage. Ryan confirmed what they had witnessed. None of them said a word for a moment, overwhelmed by emotion.

"Alex, call Robert, please. I informed him last night of my intention to come here. The FBI's criminal division should take over the investigation, starting with a bomb squad to sweep the place. This is officially a crime scene: four people have been murdered, including two law officers from this town," Ryan declared.

"Four people?" Alex and Leila both exclaimed.

With the fast chain of events and the news of Pete's death, they had forgotten about the corpses they had glimpsed on the bunker floor before the explosion.

"Yes," Jack answered. "Pete and Officer Edward, killed in the explosion, and Sheriff Walters and Nurse Brody, shot dead, their corpses disposed of in the bunker. It's their blood that's soaking our clothes."

"Alex, please also inform Robert about Beth Walters's disappearance. We don't know if she has been kidnapped or killed and her body disposed of someplace else, or if she played a more active role in these murders and is on the run. Finding her is a top priority for resolving these crimes," Ryan added.

Ryan, Jack, and Alex left the day after, accompanying Pete's body back to Washington. As Leila had guessed, Ryan had a few broken ribs, but taken as a whole, he and Jack had been incredibly lucky. By working together, they had lifted and moved several boxes at a time, unknowingly avoiding triggering the mechanism of an explosive lodged between them.

Leila had stayed behind a few more days and attended a vigil to honor those who had lost their lives in the ordeal. Ralph was remembered as a good man, always ready to help those in need, even at no cost if necessary. Several people told touching stories about times when he had made a difference in their lives. Sheriff Walters was remembered as a man of valor, proud of the position he had exerted with authority. Officer Edward was heralded as a gentle soul who had issued more warnings than tickets in his short police officer career. And Pete was described as a man who had sacrificed his life helping people he hadn't even known a few weeks before. God's forgiveness was implored for Nurse Brody.

Standing beside Leila, an elderly woman from the assisted living facility commented, "Nursing was not in her blood. She never showed compassion for those suffering. However, no one had ever thought she could be an arsonist and a cold-blooded murderer."

In any other circumstance, Leila would have admired the clouds' amazing shapes during her flight back to Houston. However, she could not let her imagination run wild; she was in a very somber mood. She was deeply affected by Pete's and Officer Edward's death and the indefinite postponement of the quest to find the other children. She was also sad about leaving the friends she had made over the few but intense days, including Ryan. He had grown on her, and she could not hold a grudge against him anymore for how he had first treated her.

PART TWO

CHAPTER 11

Thanksgiving

Vermont, November 27, 2036

THE ATMOSPHERE WAS joyful on that Thanksgiving Day. Ryan, Jack, Alex, and Leila were back at the farm. Jeff had announced a few minutes earlier that the meal would be served and invited them to take their places at the table. The aroma emanating from the kitchen was tantalizing and promised a delicious meal.

Stephan entered the dining room, beating a small drum with colorful drumsticks, followed by Martha carrying a large serving dish that she placed in the center of the table. She removed the dish cover in a theatrical gesture to expose a huge rainbow trout on lemon slices and a rice mound that was surrounded by several smaller trout leaning against its side, giving the impression of a fish merry-go-round. The bottom of the dish was covered with fresh thyme, oregano, and parsley.

"Lady and gentlemen, I present to you Big Mouth, the biggest trout from our pond, Stephan's proud catch," Martha said.

Admirative exclamations and a round of applause followed, directed toward Martha for such an artistic creation and a proudly smiling Stephan for his successful catch. As they savored several meal courses, Stephan told them, in the pure tradition of an expert fisherman, how he had finally caught Big Mouth with the help of his father. Martha teased them about the authenticity of specific details, notably the fish's extraordinary size, which must have drastically shrunk during cooking. Following suit, Alex bragged about his own sporting achievements. Considering that he didn't have the athletic body required for such prowess, his wild exaggerations resulted in some hilarious and amazing stories.

At the end of the meal, Martha took Leila aside and told her in a voice charged with emotion, "I am so grateful to you. The wonderful moments I am experiencing with Jeff and Stephen and this reunion with our most precious friends would not have been possible if it hadn't been for you. This is all your doing, Leila."

"Martha, helping you out has been the most rewarding period of my life. I wish I could have such a drastic impact on people's lives more often," Leila sincerely answered, thinking how her regular consulting routine had felt meaningless the past few months.

"Perhaps I could help you achieve that goal at least once again, if you still want to get involved in the misfortune of this village."

"Did Stephan remember any facts that might help us solve the other kidnappings?" Leila said, hopeful.

"No, but you might want to talk to Ross. His son was kidnapped five years ago, and his wife mentioned to me that he dreamed that he shared stargazing moments with his son. He'll be at the town celebration tonight. I will introduce you."

The town was the focal point of the Thanksgiving celebration. Folks from all over the county were there to participate or enjoy the live music and the singing contest. Santa Claus had just arrived in a horse-drawn carriage, children were running around, and everyone was looking forward to the much-anticipated fireworks that would take place later in the evening. Martha took Leila by the arm and navigated the crowd until she finally spotted an odd couple: a vivacious woman fully immersed in the spirit of the festivity and her morose mate, who seemed miles away.

"Patti, Ross, I am so happy to see you," Martha said, hugging them both. Then, without giving them time to answer, she went on. "You certainly remember Leila. She's visiting us for Thanksgiving. She is fascinated by the constellations shining so brightly in our night sky. It's a rare feast for the eyes of a city girl! Ross, you have such an in-depth knowledge of astronomy. Without taking too much of your time, could you name some of these stars?"

Ross initially seemed slightly surprised by Martha's request, but he quickly realized it would give him a perfect excuse to leave the joyous gathering, which starkly contrasted his feelings.

"I think I can even do better," he said. "Would you mind missing this celebration? A meteor shower is expected soon. It will be a real treat. We can observe it from my house."

"I'd love to. I've never seen such a thing, but I don't want to impose and keep you away from the festivities," Leila replied.

"You have no idea how this will please him," Patti mentioned. "I forced him to come with me. He wanted to stay home and spend the night looking through his telescope."

The prospect of watching what was dear to his heart had brought back a smile to Ross's face. He was visibly relieved to leave the noise and action behind.

They reached Ross's home fifteen minutes later, and he quickly went inside to fetch a large telescope.

"It's a beautiful night, ideal for stargazing. I'll try not to bore you with my description of the stars. Just let me know when you want to go back to town," he said, his eyes shining in anticipation of the treat nature would soon offer them.

"I'll love this. I have never had the opportunity to look at the sky through a telescope."

"The sky has fascinated me all my life. I spent much time with my son Michael studying the stars, even in the dead of winter. I promised him, for his sixteenth birthday, a trip to the Hawaiian Observatory."

He paused, overwhelmed by emotion. Silence filled the air. Then, taking a deep breath, he added sadly, "Michael was kidnapped five years ago; he turned sixteen last week."

Leila put her hand on his arm. Deep down, she could feel his pain and unwillingness to accept the ultimate finality.

"Ross, you are still strongly connected with Michael, aren't you?" Leila said.

"What do you mean?"

"You believe he is still alive. In fact, over the years, you have seen him age and become an adolescent through multiple dreams in which you talk to him, encourage him to stay strong, and tell him that one day you will be reunited again."

Ross looked at Leila intensely.

"I remember people saying you were special and could read other people's minds. I didn't think it was possible." A sad smile appeared on his lips. "In any case, as they all say, these dreams are more than likely a way of dealing with my loss."

He paused and cleared his throat before adding, "I never told anyone but Patti about those dreams, and only the first few times it happened. It pained and hurt her so much to imagine Michael alive, somewhere, in the hands of some evil kidnapper. She'd rather believe he's dead. It's her way of dealing with her grief and moving on. So, I don't mention my dreams anymore, but they never stopped. I had one last week on Michael's birthday."

Then, looking at the stars, he said, transfigured, "In these dreams, we are stargazing together, but the stars are stars only seen in the Northern sky. Last week, the northern lights illuminated the sky. We were so happy to be together, witnessing such natural beauty. Then I woke up, and it took me a moment to remember that this was just a dream," he added sadly.

"Ross, would you mind if I scan your memory to get more details from these dreams?"

"You don't need to do that. These are precious moments for me. I write down the date and draw a map of the sky that I update according to the seasons and the location of the planets."

He had brought a small box with the telescope containing an essential maintenance kit. Underneath the top section was a handwritten manual with the folded sky maps he had drawn.

"Why does this interest you?" he asked.

"Because I believe you are right; your son is alive, and these maps can help us find him," Leila replied gently, staring straight into his eyes, trying to assure him of her sincerity.

He didn't answer. His eyes filled with tears as a small glimmer of hope of finding Michael made its way into his mind. All those years of silence, doubt, joyous dreams, and sad reality must have tortured him. Behind him, Leila saw the first meteor fall, soon followed by several others. Silently, she made a wish upon a shooting star that her quest would be crowned with success.

They returned to the festivities as the fireworks unfolded. Ross wasn't convinced it would be possible to locate Michael, but he was now at peace with himself. He had better control of his emotions and no longer believed he was mentally deranged. A glimmer of hope was blooming in him now, transforming his attitude.

They found Patti with the Clarks. Ross kissed her warmly, leaving her stunned. Leila saw tears in Patti's eyes, the hope that Ross could let go, accept, and heal, and the hope that love without constant turmoil would be part of their life once more.

Ryan was talking to Joe close by. Leila joined them.

"Good evening, Joe. How are you doing? Seeing you, I realize I did not see Willie tonight. I hope he's not sick."

"No, he's fine. He's spending Thanksgiving with my brother and his family."

"And let me guess; everyone will be coming here to spend Christmas and New Year's Day with you."

"No. Only Willie. My brother and I are estranged. I haven't seen him in years. I don't even know where he is now, and I never bothered asking my dad."

Martha's arrival interrupted their conversation.

"Did you see the meteor shower?" she asked Leila. Then, pointing toward Ross, lovingly holding Patti's hands, she murmured, "I can't wait for you to tell me what you did to bring him out of his darkness."

CHAPTER 12

Robert's Unexpected Drop-in

November 28

THE FOLLOWING DAY, Leila recounted her conversation with Ross over a generous brunch of fresh bread, homemade jams, and a freshly baked quiche. She concluded, "Alex, can you pinpoint a location if you have maps of stars' position and aurora borealis with specific dates over five years?"

"I have never conducted such an analysis. With such a load of information, I can certainly identify a region, but I'm not sure I can pinpoint an exact location. It's definitely worth investigating.

"Leila, do you think Michael is still alive? Were you able to contact him?" Martha asked, excited by such an eventuality.

"Yes, I think Michael is still alive. Ross's dreams occur when specific events trigger Michael's memory of the deep relationship he shared with his father. However, even if I can connect with Michael, I would not necessarily be able to locate him unless I could see some specific landmarks. I think, in this case, the maps are our best chance."

They were interrupted by a knock at the door, and to their surprise, Robert stepped inside.

"I heard you folks were celebrating and decided to stop by," he said laughing, then turning toward Martha, he added, "I am sorry I couldn't make it yesterday—I was wrapping up a case."

They hugged him and updated him on what was going on in their lives. After a while, Leila couldn't resist asking him, "How is the investigation on the murders at the old man's house going?"

"The medical examiner has concluded that Nurse Brody had died a day before Sheriff Walters. The ballistic analysis confirmed that they were shot with the same gun used on you—the marks on the bullets matching those on the shell my team recovered in the hotel garden," Robert answered.

"Oh," murmured Leila, distressed. "She might be my assailant." She had perceived her attacker as a man, and if true, it would be the first time her perception skills had failed her. She couldn't bear the thought of such an eventuality. Could she trust her perception anymore?

"We also found DNA evidence proving Stephan and some of the other kidnapped children had been detained in the bunker. The explosives and the same fire accelerant used in the assisted living facility were in a shed near the garage, and we found the same drug used on the janitor, the nurse, and Willie in the house," Robert added.

"So, Beth Walters could be the mastermind behind Ralph's murder and Willie's attempted murder. Nurse Brody might have followed her instructions and confronted her afterward, prompting her assassination," Alex said.

"And Sheriff Walters might have guessed the bunker's location and suspected his wife's involvement. So, he tried to derail our investigation because he wanted to question her before we intervened. He might have also found Nurse Brody's body. For either or both reasons, Beth killed him," completed Jack.

"So, you now have some evidence that Beth Walters might be Leila's attacker, the mastermind behind the children's kidnappings, and a serial killer, but you still cannot exclude the fact that she might have been framed, killed, and her body disposed of someplace else," Ryan resumed. "As I said months ago, these crimes cannot be resolved until we find her. Any clue where she is now?"

"No, she vanished. She must have switched cars or license plates, and we couldn't locate her even with our most sophisticated recognition software. To make matters worse, we do not have any recent pictures; her driver's license is decades old, and she has rarely been seen in recent years. Sketches were drawn based on people's memories, but they are inaccurate, and as usual, the witnesses contradict each other.

"If she is what we think she might be, she certainly does not want to be found. She must have used an invisible cloak to escape detection," Alex added.

"Alex, what are you talking about? Are you referring to the invisible cloak used by Harry Potter? You realize that's a fictional story, don't you?" Ryan said.

"No Ryan, I'm not fantasizing. Some pattern designs confuse and neutralize recognition software. They can be part of a hat, a T-shirt, a dress, or can be drawn on a face. It's well known in the world of informatics. They are and were previously used by some protesters in countries like Hong Kong where the government monitored the whereabouts of its citizens and cracked down on dissent," Alex corrected.

"This may sound odd, Alex, but could you develop a reverse recognition software that doesn't search for specific individuals but tracks those it cannot identify?" Leila asked.

"That's a brilliant idea. It will take time, but it might work. I'll work on it as soon as I'm done savoring this delicious brunch."

Apart from brief appearances at mealtimes where he was lost in his thoughts, Alex spent the rest of the day and Saturday in his room. However, in the wee hours of Sunday morning, when everyone was still asleep, he knocked on each bedroom door shouting, "I found her, I found her."

They gathered in the living room, half awake, still struggling against the fog clouding their minds. Nevertheless, Alex took less than a minute to catch their full attention, as his excitement was contagious.

"Leila's idea to modify my recognition software was brilliant. I first narrowed my search to Vermont and captured her leaving the village by herself. She has not been kidnapped. I followed her from place to place. She headed west. I've traced her up to Pennsylvania so far. It's a slow process, but it's doable. I'll be able to pinpoint where she is, and we'll just have to pick her up."

"It's fantastic, Alex," Robert exclaimed. "Please authorize us and tell us how to operate your modified software—and transfer all the info you have so far to my people so we can take over and pursue the search from now on."

"Let's team up," Ryan said.

"I'm sorry, Ryan, but Beth Walters is more than likely a serial killer. She falls under my jurisdiction. Moreover, this case is too personal for you and your team to be involved. I will keep you posted on any developments," Robert replied.

"You bet it's personal," Ryan said with apparent bitterness. "She killed Pete, one of my men, a loyal friend who didn't deserve to die this way. Every day reminds me of him. Finding her is my only way to come to terms with Pete's death, to get closure. I won't let you push me out of this investigation so easily. I—"

To everyone's surprise, Alex interrupted the confrontation between the two men. In a calm and conciliatory voice, he said, "I thought you might say so, Robert. Your team will find everything they need in this external drive. They can contact me if they need my help."

Silence filled the room. Then, without hesitation, Robert took the external drive from Alex's hand.

"Greatly appreciated, Alex. Thank you for your understanding."

And without looking at Ryan, he stormed out of the room to get dressed and pack his belongings. No one moved or said a single word. Ryan's anger was palpable. He stood and walked in front of a window, his fists clenched. It was easy to imagine him punching the adjacent wall to relieve his fury.

Robert was in his car less than ten minutes later, already on the phone rallying his team. As soon as Robert's car door closed, Ryan turned to Alex, who was unusually quiet and unflustered, and said, "If you want me to spare your life, tell me that this external drive is pure bullshit, that you already know where Beth is."

"Did Leila teach you to read minds?" Alex teased.

"It's not a good time to mess with my nerves, Alex. In any case, I can't see you willingly agreeing to be cavalierly pushed aside and let others be credited for your work unless you have something major up your sleeve."

A smirk appeared on Alex's lips. "I focused my efforts on triangulating Ross's information and was able to pinpoint the location where the kids might be. Then, I spent minimal time updating the software and searching for Beth, just enough to corroborate that she was heading in that direction."

Ryan shook his head, and a mischievous expression matching Alex's smile appeared, erasing all traces of anger and aggression.

"So, we all agree. Officially, we will focus on the children's rescue. Kidnapping is in our mandate. Robert does not have to be involved in this investigation. If we inadvertently catch Beth in our nets, we'll take care of her. Now Alex, where are the children and Beth, most likely?"

"In Alaska. Only one inhabitable isolated location is visible on satellite imagery."

CHAPTER 13

Anchorage, Alaska

December 2

THREE DAYS LATER, Ryan, Alex, Jack, and Leila landed in Anchorage, where a frigid twelve degrees Fahrenheit temperature welcomed them. It was a shock, especially for Leila; the cold air penetrated through her inadequate clothing, freezing her to the bone. She pulled the collar up on her coat and shivered uncontrollably.

Seeing her misery, Ryan smiled and exhaled a puff of air that immediately condensed before his mouth.

"Don't you like walking on a cloud?" he said teasingly. "Don't worry, you'll get used to the cold. In a few days, you may even consider this a balmy temperature. It will be much colder where we are going."

"Thanks, Ryan. It's truly heartwarming!" Leila replied, happy to jump in the heated car waiting outside the terminal to drive them to the Alaska commissioner's office.

Hoping to get more information on the location Alex had triangulated, Ryan had contacted Commissioner Johnston the day before and had informed her that many abducted children were being held in Alaska. The shocking allegation had lifted the usual administrative red tape when scheduling a meeting on such short notice.

The commissioner's assistant ushered them into a room filled with spectacular photos of Alaska's wildlife and mountains. A small woman in business attire, with short black hair, was seated behind an enormous wooden desk, which, by contrast, gave her a fragile appearance. She stood up to shake their hands vigorously. The willpower that emanated from her conveyed a clear message to take her seriously. She addressed them with a firm and authoritative voice.

"Welcome to Anchorage."

Then, talking to Ryan specifically, she pointed to two officials standing respectfully behind her.

"Agent Steele, after reviewing the document you sent me, I took the liberty of inviting Chief Bert Hilton, the Anchorage chief of police, and Marshal James White."

Leila sensed submission and apprehension in both officers, but the commissioner didn't give her time to delve into what was at the root of their feelings. She immediately resumed, emphasizing her unspoken opinion through specific words. "If I understand correctly, you believe that abducted children have been concealed and enslaved in Alaska for almost a decade. Since you do not have strong evidence to support such a conclusion, it is, at the moment, only speculation. How can we help restore our state's good reputation in your mind?"

"Can you tell us what you know about the suspected location?" Ryan asked, ignoring the commissioner's allegation that his claim was pure fantasy and that he was, per deduction, unqualified for his job.

"This was the site of a small town, a relic of the gold rush, which boomed in size overnight with mining development. The place was abandoned, and the site was bought ten years ago by a consortium named AgroFuture. At the time of purchase, the company stated that the mine's infrastructure would be used for hydroponic agriculture, a proprietary technology developed for this purpose."

"Has AgroFuture fulfilled its claim?"

"Absolutely. It dominates the Alaskan fruit and vegetable market and has since expanded beyond the state border."

"How many people does the company employ in Alaska?"

"Only a handful at the Anchorage office and on-site."

"Has anyone ever inspected or visited the facility?"

"Chief?" Commissioner Johnston answered. Her voice sounded like an order, or at least the permission to speak.

"It was inspected before it became operational. Most of its operations are computerized and robotized. A journalist also did an inquiry a few years ago," Chief Hilton answered. "She published a great article on the installation."

"Was there any contact with any of the employees?"

"Those working on location are very isolated. We have never seen them. They live in modern installations surrounding the mine. They are self-sufficient. The company owns a plane to transport its produce to Anchorage and fly back whatever the facility needs. We never had any complaints. We have no reason to go there and investigate," Marshall White replied.

"The few employees working in the Anchorage office keep to themselves," Chief Hilton added. "Not even a speeding ticket. They are exemplary citizens."

"Agent Steele, as you can see, we have no reason to investigate either the AgroFuture Anchorage office or the on-site facility. I cannot authorize any legal inquisition, let alone a police raid," Commissioner Johnston said, regaining control of the conversation. "What are your intentions?" Her tone sounded more like a thinly veiled threat of retaliation than a request to elaborate on their plan.

"Don't worry; no illegal actions will be taken against AgroFuture. We will inform you if we find out they are implicated in any criminal wrongdoings. However, I would request that you keep this meeting and the purpose of our presence confidential. If our deductions are correct, we don't want to arouse their suspicion," Ryan replied, sustaining the commissioner's stare.

Then, without any handshake, Ryan turned around and left the office. The team followed closely behind, not without wondering how he had kept in check his short-fused temper and not lashed out at the commissioner.

Leila was warming up slowly, wrapped in a blanket and drinking a delicious hot chocolate. They were gathered in the living room of the house they had rented in the suburb of Anchorage. Alex was alternately projecting tridimensional maps of Alaska and AgroFuture installations in the center of the room. Jack was carefully studying both maps. Ryan was standing, obviously still angry, a few feet from one of the room's corners, his arms crossed tightly across his chest, his towering stature producing an impressive shadow on the wall behind him.

"I think we have disturbed the tranquility of the Alaskan authorities. We must now be on their list of potential troublemakers," Alex said, expressing everyone's thoughts.

"What concerns them is not so much their tranquility as the bad publicity that can endanger their political careers," Ryan said. "Don't worry about it. What did you find?"

"The AgroFuture facility is in the northeastern part of the state. The easiest way to get there is by plane. They have a small adjacent airstrip that is well maintained. Wilderness surrounds the complex," Alex answered.

"Perfect location to detain people against their will," Jack commented.

"Better yet, the site is gated and guarded by electronic surveillance. On closer inspection, there appears also to be a defense arsenal. So, if unannounced and unwanted visitors are detected, they could face life-threatening injuries if they persist in their approach," Alex added.

"So, the state authority will not help in any way, and we cannot raid the facility. What's left?" Jack asked.

"The facts are that as federal government employees, you have a strict code of conduct to abide by, but, as a civilian, I have more *flexibility*. Conversely, you have the legal authority to rescue me if I am distressed. Don't you?" Leila said.

"I'm far from sure I like the direction this conversation is taking," Ryan replied.

CHAPTER 14

Plan of Action

Anchorage, December 3

JORDAN BERGMAN, THE Anchorage journalist who'd written the article on AgroFuture, worked as a freelancer. Leila contacted her, introducing herself as an investigator for a firm interested in investing in or possibly buying AgroFuture. This piqued the journalist's interest, and, hoping to get a scoop on the business acquisition, she agreed to meet at a coffee shop.

Jordan was in her early thirties. Not particularly beautiful, she was nonetheless charming, visibly fit, and energetic. While drinking hot chocolate, her beverage of choice in Alaska, Leila was now listening to her story, which turned out to be quite different from what Chief Hilton had let them believe.

"I had contacted the AgroFuture office in Anchorage on several occasions. Since no one was returning my calls, I went directly to their facility to get an interview with the chief operating officer and possibly have a tour of their installation. In my job, you cannot wait indefinitely for people to have the decency to get back to you."

Leila nodded, reassuring Jordan she understood her perspective: she wasn't a quiet and withdrawn person—she pushed her luck to get what she wanted.

"So here I was, miles away from all civilization, at the gates of their facility, an inoffensive woman, politely asking to speak to the director of operations, identifying myself as a journalist. I was obviously not there to spy or destroy anything. Well, not only did the guards refuse to let me speak to their supervisor, but they also threatened to shoot me if I didn't leave immediately."

"Then, how were you able to write your article?"

"My little excursion finally caught the attention of the Anchorage office. Their administrator contacted me. He told me I should never have gone to their facility without authorization. The guards are humanoid robots programmed to deny entry to anyone. Between you and me, I think they're programmed to shoot and leave people bleeding and freezing to death outside their gate if they don't manage to kill them first."

"So you finally got the authorization to visit their site."

"No, they sent me a video of a virtual tour of the facility, the type produced for investors or publicity."

"Oh! But something still bothers you, even after all these years, apart from the fact that these are distrustful people who fear intruders."

"I didn't know I was so easy to read," she said, smiling.

Leila smiled back but didn't comment.

Jordan went on. "They have computers monitoring the light, temperature, water, nutrients, and growth of their crop. They have robots harvesting their produce. They have humanoids guarding the facility. I may be overreacting to how humans have become obsolete in their organization, but they must have at least a few employees; all cannot be done without human supervision or with only one director of operations. There wasn't a single employee in their video," she said, frustrated.

"The eradication of humans by AI! This has been the subject of several philosophical articles. However, I see you as a practical person," Leila said, looking at Jordan intently.

Jordan held her gaze, debating whether to reveal what she had found. She finally added, "Their products are brought to Anchorage by plane. Once again, without a pilot. The aircraft is equipped for automated takeoff and landing and has a programmed flight plan. The aircraft can be remotely controlled like a drone, if required. After it lands, an Anchorage employee controls a robot that empties it and loads the van for distribution. The plane is then loaded back with whatever the facility needs. I watched the entire process from afar a few times using binoculars. Once, one of the crates fell, and its content spilled onto the tarmac."

Jordan paused to emphasize her next statement.

"It contained several boxes of toothpaste, sanitary tampons and pads, and toilet paper. The amount they shipped would take a single person years to go through."

"What?" Leila exclaimed.

"Exactly. It doesn't add up. If most of the AgroFuture workforce is made up of robots, what are all these hygiene products needed for?"

"You never mentioned this in your article or to anyone?"

"I would have been obliged to acknowledge and explain why I was spying on them. Moreover, the purchase of these products does not constitute a criminal offense. Alaskans are proud of this local business. We now have fresh farm produce. I would have risked my career by discrediting AgroFuture for toilet paper rolls, toothpaste, and tampons!"

Jordan was right. However, her observation and the mystery surrounding the facility supported the team's conclusion that the abducted children might be held at AgroFuture.

"Do you still have, by any chance, the facility's video?" Leila asked her.

"Yes. I will lend it to you if you promise exclusivity on any deal your firm will make or give me your impression of AgroFuture, its employees, and installations if you can visit the facility in person."

"Agreed." Leila smiled and shook Jordan's hand.

Leila knew that Jordan had no idea what the real impact of her bargain was, but when the time came, she would be happy to give her the scoop on what was really behind the facade of AgroFuture. It would catapult Jordan's career for sure.

"I have my admission ticket," Leila said back at the house, proudly flaunting the video she had acquired.

"What did you find?" Jack asked.

"If we watch this video carefully, we'll find out where the AgroFuture robots were assembled," she replied.

"How does this concern us?" Jack asked.

"Robots occasionally need an inspection, fine-tuning, and an upgrade. You can officially request that the robotic company issue a plausible recommended action for a critical repair and teach me how to fix the robots. I can introduce myself as the robotic technician to the AgroFuture folks in Anchorage's office and convince them I need to go on-site for repairs and upgrades. Once there, I will confirm the presence of the children. This should be enough for you to intervene legally."

"You really believe I'm going to send you, an untrained civilian, to a dangerous and isolated place where you could be killed before we even have time to intervene? Get real!" Ryan said.

"There's a simple and good reason why I must go there," Leila argued defiantly. "Do you think AgroFuture management will ever graciously introduce the children to any of you? Get real! I am the only one who can perceive their presence and communicate with them telepathically."

"Time out," Alex cut in. "I don't want to disillusion either of you about the importance of the role you could play, but any mechanical update or fine-tuning of a robot requires informatic reprogramming and testing. Any respectable company would send a technician and an informatician for such work. So, you need me to keep up appearances. Once there, I can hack their system to access their facility operation."

"It's perfect; the icing on the cake. While you're both at it, why not go there with a painted bullseye on your back?" Ryan said, exasperated and frustrated by the logic and accuracy of their arguments.

CHAPTER 15

AgroFuture Facility

December 10

THE COMPANY THAT manufactured the robots for AgroFuture agreed to cooperate after Ryan "kindly" suggested that a refusal to do so could be unfavorably perceived if AgroFuture's illegal operations were to be confirmed. Its maintenance service department contacted the AgroFuture office to offer them, free of charge, as part of the annual maintenance agreement, an essential upgrade to fix a bug and avoid a possible robotic malfunction in the near future. Its engineers briefly trained Leila and Alex to carry out a credible repair.

A week later, Leila and Alex boarded the AgroFuture plane retrofitted with two seats. Other than them and the equipment they carried, the plane's cargo bay was empty. Leila hesitantly buckled her seat belt, staring uncomfortably at the closed piloting cabin door. Amazingly, she was more concerned about the lack of a pilot than their visit to the facility. However, except for some strong turbulence, the flight went well, and they landed safely and soundly. An imposing man with the physical features of a wrestler and a blank expression on his face was waiting for them upon arrival.

"Art, chief operating officer," was his glacial welcome, keeping with the temperature. One could easily deduce that human relationships were not his forte. Moreover, his handshake was on the edge of what Leila considered physically tolerable. She refrained from wincing, but for a moment, she thought he would crush her bones.

Without further introductions, Art indicated they should take their places with their equipment in an open four-seater Jeep better suited for an African safari than the Alaskan winter and drove toward a nearby well-lit tunnel opposite a cluster of houses. The tunnel was impressive: big enough for a mega-truck to drive in. Inside, a large platform adjacent to a railroad track, several old mine carts, and a locomotive could be seen. Leila's face must have reflected her astonishment.

"Yes, these antiques are still in use. They are handy for certain tasks," Art said before Leila could even question him, proving that he was watching their reactions.

They drove down an inclined path heading below ground. They reached two large, laminated glass doors that Art remotely opened. An immense illuminated cave appeared in front of them. The freezing Alaskan temperature, the solid rock walls and ceiling, and the absence of sun and clouds all faded. Leila saw rows of various fruits and vegetable crops, flowers, and bees gathering nectar in well-tended cultivated soil, bathing in the dim light of a nice summer day.

"Bees? You have bees?" Leila exclaimed, snapping back to the reality of the underground cave.

"Yes, we need them to pollinate, and people love our honey. We keep the beehives in a separate cave."

"How do you keep them inside when the doors open?" Alex asked.

"You probably haven't noticed it, but a weak magnetic field keeps them away from the doors."

They drove along the cave wall, moving away from the doors. They entered the adjacent cave, where ten picking robots were gathered.

"The robots are yours for the day. Number One is at your service if you need anything." Art indicated.

"Number One?" Leila asked.

"We have different robots depending on their role. Artificial Intelligence Number One or AI-One is used for communication and service. If Number One cannot address your needs, it will transmit them to the Control Center and, therefore, to me. Bathroom facilities and a kitchenette with water and food are in the back of this cave." Seeing her surprise, he added, "We need them to accommodate our rare guests. I will let you work now. I will see you later."

They immediately started working on the first robot. Their conversation was focused on their work to give a professional impression and appease any suspicion. With Number One omnipresent, all their movements were most likely transmitted to a central post where Art could watch them.

At the end of the morning, they went to the kitchenette for lunch, Number One on their heels. Fresh fruit lined a large table. As Leila was putting a variety of berries and grapes on her plate, a few fell, and she had to crawl under the table to chase after them. Careful not to hit her head on the table, she looked up as she came out. To her surprise, she saw a small piece of paper taped to the side of the interior panel of the table in a place where, if someone had pulled a chair closer using the table to assist them, their hand would have touched it. Intrigued, she put her hand on the inside panel as if to stabilize herself and grabbed the paper, unnoticed by Number One. She slipped it into her jeans pocket and emerged from under the table.

After lunch, Leila went to the bathroom. She retrieved the paper, hiding it and its contents with her body in case there was a hidden camera. Words had been written with what seemed to be strawberry juice on silky paper commonly used to wrap peaches: *HELP! ABDUCTED!* Based on the vibrant color of the words, the note was recent. She sighed in relief. The children were indeed here, alive, and at least one of them was resilient and still fighting back against the tyranny of his captor. She telepathically transmitted the information to Ryan.

It took them the rest of the day to fix all the robots. As they were wrapping up, Number One projected a tridimensional hologram of Art, "I see you're almost done. Everything went well?"

"Your robots are fully functional. We did a test run, and they successfully picked up fragile items of different sizes without damaging them. You shouldn't have any problem," Alex replied.

"We're ready to go," Leila added.

"Unfortunately, it will not be possible for you to leave the facility tonight. The weather has turned into a blizzard. You will have to spend the night here. I'll send you the Jeep, and Number One will drive you to a house where you will spend the night. Don't worry; our guest house has all the necessary comforts. You should be able to leave tomorrow morning."

It was already dark when the Jeep came out of the mine. Even with the streetlights, visibility was reduced to a few feet. The contrast between the controlled environment of the caves and the outside temperature was brutal. Their open vehicle took at least four long minutes at low speed to reach the house that would be their refuge for the night. Number One dropped them there, and the car drove away. Once again, Leila had never been so glad to enter a warm room.

They found everything they needed for the night, from a toothbrush to flannel pajamas. A light dinner had also been prepared, and they devoured it. Alex then retired to his bedroom. Gathering her courage, Leila decided to explore their surroundings, hoping to locate where the children were being held. To her dismay, the door was locked, and she couldn't find any controls to unlock it.

Alex must have heard her shuffling around in all the drawers she could find. He came to her, and before Leila could explain what she was looking for, he said, "I know, we're locked up. However, it won't be for long. I hacked their system. Let me show you the whole infrastructure. Currently, there are two locked houses. The closest to the mine entrance could be where the children are held, and based on the time it took us to get here, this must be our house."

"Can you unlock them?"

"Yes, easily done, but I don't want to activate an alarm while doing so. I am finalizing a script to put me in charge of the entire security. I am now feeding their system with false information; there is no longer any visual or audio recording live from inside this house."

"Oh, of course," Leila said. "I had been so focused on the children that the thought of us being monitored hadn't crossed my mind. What about the service robots?"

"Another hour, and I'll gain full control. It's a bit more complicated than the security, but I worked on it while we were in the cave. I tested the script a few times on Number One this afternoon by giving it a few commands."

"Ah, that explains its unusual jerky movements. Let me know when you'll be ready for a walk in the tropics. I'll retire to my bedroom in the meantime."

CHAPTER 16

Michael

December 10

RYAN HAD PROVIDED them with computer-generated sketches of the children who had gone missing in recent years in the Springtown area. Their current facial features had been extrapolated from photos taken before their abduction. Michael's sketch was of the highest quality, drawn under Ross's directive, and based on his most recent dreamed encounters with his son. The purpose of these sketches was not only to help them identify the children but to facilitate, in Leila's case, telepathic interaction by allowing her to visualize them. This was especially true for Michael, who she believed would be the most receptive to telepathy. She was also willing to bet that Michael was the author of the desperate note she had found. So, she focused on his facial features and pictured him in a room like the one she was in now, lying in bed, hoping the strangers visiting the facility had found his note and could free him and his companions.

Suddenly, Leila visualized the ceiling of a room. It was dark indigo and sparkled with a multitude of white dots. In a flash, she recognized some of the patterns created by the bright spots: the star constellations of the sky in Vermont that Ross had shown her. A feeling of gratification washed over her; she was connected with Michael.

"Michael, I'm Leila. I found your message. I can help you."

His first reaction was skepticism. He thought he was daydreaming.

"I'm real, Michael. We can communicate telepathically, as you do with your dad when you look at the sky and the northern lights and share your impressions and feelings with him."

By relating his dreamlike interactions with his father, Michael became more at ease with the possibility that Leila could mentally communicate with him. However, it was difficult for him to communicate with a stranger he had never seen.

"I'm on-site with a friend. We'll go to your house later tonight. I'll let you know when we're on our way. You'll then be able to join us outside; your door will be unlocked."

Alex finally took control of the outdoor video surveillance of the entire facility. The images were a repeat of the previous hour and were no longer transmitted live. The blizzard and reduced visibility facilitated the illusion: the blowing snow was the constancy of the hour, and it was a credible fact for anyone watching live.

Leila contacted Michael as soon as they were ready to go. They then stepped outside. Even though she expected it, the conditions were brutally cold. The wind was forcibly blowing the snow, and Leila had the unpleasant feeling of being stung in the face simultaneously by many tiny needles. They faced the storm and fought the wind and snow slowly and painfully. They finally reached the house where Michael and the other children were being held. He was waiting outside, appropriately bundled up to face the glacial weather. He motioned to follow him inside an adjacent unoccupied house.

They stepped inside a living room with a large bay window. The light from the streetlamps, reflected by the snow, illuminated the room, conferring an eerie atmosphere. The house was not heated, but it was nevertheless more comfortable than being exposed to the relentless wind and blowing snow.

Michael removed the scarf covering his face, and they were shocked to see how accurate Ross had been in his description. Still shaking from the cold, Leila initiated the conversation with a shivering voice.

"Hi Michael, I'm Leila; this is Alex. I am thrilled to meet you in person. Your father told me so much about you."

His father's invocation brought tears to his eyes, but he fought them proudly.

"You know my father? I missed him so much. You're going to free us, aren't you?"

"We won't be able to take you on the plane tomorrow, but we will return soon with reinforcement to rescue you all."

"You won't be leaving tomorrow. Two days ago, Art told us to prepare for a storm that would impact us for days. We sent all our products to Anchorage yesterday, ahead of our regular schedule. It might take another day or two before the wind calms down enough for a plane to fly."

"What?" Leila exclaimed, looking at Alex, who seemed as concerned as she was.

"The AgroFuture office staff had delayed our visit by a day. They must have already been aware of this storm," Alex said.

They had never looked at the weather forecast, busy as they were with all the preparations. But the turbulence they experienced during their flight was at the forefront of the storm.

Thinking out loud, Leila added, "My god, they wanted us to stay stuck here, at the mercy of the storm. Outside communication is even cut off."

"And there's only one explanation for that: they know our identity," Alex said, his deductions matching her thoughts.

"Do you know where Art is?" Leila asked Michael.

"I saw him load the Jeep with several suitcases and a briefcase about an hour after your arrival. He then left the Control Center and headed for the airstrip. The plane took off a few minutes later. He never came back. He must have boarded the plane."

"Are you sure? He spoke to us around five o'clock this afternoon." As Leila said this, she realized they hadn't seen him physically. "Oh! It was only a projection transmitted by Number One; he could have been miles away, or it could have been recorded hours earlier."

"You mentioned the Control Center: where is it, and what can be controlled from there?" Alex asked.

Through the window, Michael pointed at a large house farther down the street, barely visible between the gusts of wind and snow.

"Art monitors the whole facility from there."

"Can he control the ambient temperature in all houses?" Leila asked.

Both looked at her, surprised by what seemed like an irrelevant question.

"Yes," Michael answered. "Art can raise or lower temperatures as he wishes. He did it several times to show us he had full control over our lives."

Earlier at the house, while waiting for Alex to be ready, Leila had felt the ambient temperature steadily drop.

"So, we were left in a locked house, with no food other than the bit we had for dinner and no heat. A guaranteed death by hypothermia and freezing, accelerated by starvation."

"How about you?" Alex asked Michael.

"Same situation," Michael answered.

"We should go to the caves until we get rescued. It's warm there, and the food is plentiful," Alex suggested.

"The doors are locked. Art has a remote control, or they can be opened from the Control Center," Michael said.

"Well, I think we should visit the Control Center," Leila said.

Gunshots and screams interrupted their conversation. It was so unexpected that, for a moment, they all froze. Then, Michael ran out, and Alex went after him.

"Stay here," he yelled, slamming the door shut.

As Leila looked through the bay window, she saw them both disappear in a whirlwind of snow. Under other circumstances, she would have admired the magical atmosphere conferred by windblown snow, but now she could only wonder what was happening and anxiously wait for their safe return. A few minutes passed; nothing happened. She could no longer stand still, staring at the white emptiness. She took the flashlight she had found at the guesthouse out of her bag and searched for anything they could use.

CHAPTER 17

Ray of Hope

December 10

THE HOUSE SEEMED frozen in time, fully furnished and well maintained. The kitchen drawers contained a few spoons, and the cabinets had a few plates, cups, and glasses. By association, seeing these, Leila craved hot chocolate, but there was no time to waste in wishful thinking. She went on with her investigation. The bathroom cabinets were empty. There were no towels, disinfectant, or running water. The closets in the bedrooms only contained plastic hangers. However, in one of the bedrooms, a rustic wooden storage trunk stood in plain view in the center of the room. It seemed to have been loaded with clothes for an imminent departure and then forgotten. Leila opened it. Surprisingly, it contained several women's parkas and warm ski pants. For a moment, she stared at the precious contents. She felt like a gold prospector finding a huge nugget in his gold pan.

She grabbed a parka, hoping it would fit her. Before she could put it on, she heard noises coming from the front of the house. Reluctantly, she put the parka back in the trunk and returned to the living room. Alex and Michael were stepping inside, carrying a teenager about Michael's age, barely conscious and with blood staining the sleeve of his parka. From the sketches, she recognized Jason. They laid him down on the sofa. Two other teenagers, she identified as Shawn and Andrew, entered carrying towels. They must have stopped by their house before coming here. They were out of breath and visibly scared.

"Jason has been hit," Michael said, stating an obvious fact in a voice that reflected denial and anger. Then, looking at Shawn and Andrew, he asked them, "What in hell were you doing at the Control Center?"

"We saw you leaving and thought you were going to get food. We decided to follow you," Shawn replied.

"It's total devastation there," Andrew added. "The guard has pulverized all the AIs. He shot at us when we stepped inside."

"The guard?" Alex asked, puzzled.

"There are five humanoid guards, one in the Control Center and four at the perimeter wall," Michael answered. "Whereas the AI service robots transmit information, clean, maintain, and cook, the role of the guards is to protect and defend the facility. They are programmed to kill intruders if necessary. But they should not shoot at us unless we try to escape."

"Hell, I have no control over the guard," Alex said, distraught. He added, "I didn't see any program script related to them."

"There is probably one, but I don't think we have the luxury of time for you to find it and hack it," Leila said, bringing him back to reality. "The boys wandered outside their house, which should have been locked, and went undetected to the Control Center without triggering any alarm. It's now obvious to anyone in charge that the surveillance system has been tampered with and that what is being seen is not the actual reality."

"I don't understand why the guard shot at us and why he destroyed the AIs," Shawn said. Then, looking at Alex and Leila, he suddenly realized that these strangers might be the source of their problems. "Who are you? What have you done that resulted in such mayhem?"

"My name is Leila. This is Alex. We are here to rescue you," Leila said before adding, "Alex, do you know what's going on?"

"Art must have figured out that I would hack the facility system, starting with the AIs. They were destroyed, so I could not program them to help us. Based on what just happened, we can assume that the guards have been reprogrammed to let no one survive or escape, including you guys," Alex answered, pointing at the four adolescents.

"They must also be programmed to hunt us down," Leila added. "We need to get out of AgroFuture before it's too late."

"We cannot venture into this storm. At the very least, we need the Jeep," Alex said.

"It is at the Control Center," Andrew said.

"Number 1 must have brought it there after dropping us," Leila said.

"We cannot go there; it's too dangerous. Any other mode of transport?" Alex asked.

"The snowmobiles," Andrew replied.

Leila put on the clothes she had seen in the trunk and joined the others at the boys' house. They shoved flashlights, water bottles, and any food they could find into some backpacks, and the boys gave Alex some of their clothes that were warmer than those he was wearing. They dressed Jason's wound as best they could, as he tried to hide his pain.

The snowmobiles were stored, among other things, in a large building at the edge of the village, in the opposite direction of the mine, not far from the perimeter wall. To make the most of their time, Alex and Andrew went ahead, walking at a fast pace, to get the snowmobiles ready.

Michael and Shawn helped Jason, who showed signs of exhaustion, and Leila carried their backpacks. They were moving slowly, but the wind blowing on their backs pushed them, helping them progress. When they finally reached the garage, Alex and Andrew's facial expressions were grim.

"We only found one snowmobile with a full charge. The electricity is off, so we can't charge the others. Only two people can fit on it," Alex said, visibly disappointed.

"Take Jason with you," Leila said to Alex. "He needs medical attention as soon as possible before an infection sets in."

He was about to argue when Leila saw two sleds at the back of the garage. "What are those for?" she asked, pointing to them, thinking they could tie them to the snowmobile, even if it would be dangerous for their occupants.

"They're for the dogs," Andrew said.

"You have dogs, sled dogs?" Leila asked hopefully.

"We have seven dogs. I'm their caretaker. They are outside, behind this building," Shawn replied.

"That's our way out," Leila said enthusiastically.

They let Michael and Andrew prepare the sleds while Shawn and Leila went out. The dogs were curled up, shielding themselves from the wind and keeping warm. Seeing them, they got up, a glimmer of anticipation in their eyes, and their tails shot up, slowly wagging.

"We can tie three dogs to each sled. But we can't use this one. She's too vicious." Shawn pointed to a secluded enclosure where a single, beautiful Siberian Husky dog was tied to a post with a short leash. "She was the best lead dog we ever had, but she's strong-minded, and Art has beaten her senselessly. He is keeping her now for breeding only."

"What's her name?"

"Snow."

Leila approached the enclosure; Snow growled. She sat down on the ground to be at her level. Their eyes locked. Snow held her gaze but gradually calmed down. Leila smiled; Art hadn't destroyed her spirit. Keeping her eyes on her, she told Shawn, "Help Michael and Andrew prepare a three- and a four-dog sled. Snow will be the lead dog of the four-dog sled. I'll be in that sled, and you will drive it."

Shawn hesitated a few seconds. He wasn't sure if Snow could be trusted, but at the same time, Leila could see he was conflicted with his desire not to abandon her here to an undeniable fate. He finally nodded and went inside, returning a few minutes later with the sleds and Michael and Andrew. She gave them time to tie the other dogs to the sleds, then brought Snow. While they took care of her, Leila joined Alex in the garage. He was still working on his computer.

"Did you find a way to get us out of here without being killed?" Leila asked him.

"I gained control of the gate. It will open as we approach it. The rest is up to us."

"What do you have in mind?"

"The blizzard must affect the guards' visual and thermal sensors. They cannot correctly triangulate the position of their target, which is why Jason is still alive. We can confuse their sensors even more and increase our chances of survival by lowering our body temperature."

"You're suggesting we remove some clothing?"

"Yes. We would keep only a few basics, including our gloves and boots, to protect our extremities for the time it takes to be out of reach."

Leila cringed at the idea of barely shielding herself from temperatures that could induce hypothermia in minutes, but she knew they had no choice, as hazardous and crazy as it sounded. Then, a thought crossed her mind to further increase the guards' confusion.

CHAPTER 18

Mayhem

December 10–11

LEILA TOOK SNOW'S head in her hands, locked her eyes into hers, and said, "Snow, it's your time to shine. Give us a hundred percent. I'm counting on you so we can all survive and be free."

Snow's eyes reflected her willingness to prove herself. She was ready.

Leila got in the sled and lay down. Shawn crouched down on the sled's skis. Andrew and Michael followed their lead. Alex positioned the snowmobile between the two sleds, Jason seated behind him. They were the most exposed. By putting them between the two sleds, they hoped it might offer them some protection.

Leila whistled and shouted, "Go, Snow."

Snow sprinted, and the other dogs matched her speed. They went around the building and raced toward the gate. They heard gunshots, bullets ricocheting off the icy ground, the dogs' paws hitting the ground faster and faster, the metal runners of the sleds sliding on the frozen snow. Suddenly, covering all noises, an explosion erupted. From that point on, the trajectory of the bullets became totally erratic. The heat sensors of the humanoids were confused by the blizzard, the unusually low body temperatures of the group fleeing, the heat of the explosion, and the fire now raging in the garage.

Nothing was stopping Snow. She was focused on the gate that was now opening in front of her. She flew through it, and they found themselves outside the walls, free. Shawn let the dogs run for a few more minutes to reach the safe zone outside the gun-shooting perimeter, then ordered them to stop. None of them had been hit. The boys were excited, screaming at the top of their lungs.

"Clothes back on, everyone, before you freeze to death," Leila said. Then, seeing Jason's white face, she said, "Go ahead, Alex, full speed."

"I'll return with the team, and we'll find you."

"Don't worry, Alex, we won't be far behind you," Leila said.

He smiled to comfort them, well aware that their chances of survival were far less than his. He waved, and the snowmobile soon disappeared toward the closest agglomeration, miles away. The sled led by Snow followed the same path.

About an hour later, Snow suddenly stopped, growled, and refused to follow Shawn's command to move on. Her whole attitude suddenly turned aggressive.

"I'm going to see why Snow is behaving like this," Leila told Shawn, getting out of the sled.

"Be careful; she might bite you. I'm not sure we can trust her," he said, afraid of Snow.

As Leila walked toward Snow, she sensed nervousness and fear in the other three dogs tied behind her.

"Snow, what's wrong, girl? Tell me."

Snow briefly turned her head toward Leila, which was enough for Leila to know what she and the other dogs had smelled. Leila's skin bristled under her thick layer of clothing. She began to remove Snow's harness quickly. She turned to Shawn and the others and yelled, "Quick, untie all the dogs. NOW."

They seemed surprised by her order, but the authoritarian tone of her voice prompted them to act without further hesitation. Leila had barely finished releasing Snow when she heard a low growl. A giant polar bear appeared in the twilight, obviously in the hunt for food. It was too close for comfort. It lifted itself on its hind legs and then propelled itself toward them. Snow charged at it. They met halfway. Snow bit its snout, then narrowly avoided its fangs and a blow from its enormous paw. Under Snow's leadership, the other dogs, now acting as a pack, attacked. The battle was fierce, the dogs circling the bear, biting its rear legs, then moving away from the reach of its claws. A dog was hit hard, but Snow counterattacked and bit the bear in the neck. The bear's energetic nod sent her flying several yards away. Within seconds, she was back on her feet again and resumed her place in the fight.

The humans watched the battle helpless and scared.

Suddenly, the bear, frustrated by such a fierce and relentless attack, retreated, pursued by the dogs. Shawn grabbed his backpack and ran to the injured dog, lying motionless on the slowly reddening snow around him. He knelt by his side and petted him. The dog emitted a faint sound. Shawn carefully lifted the dog's head and kissed it. Then, with a sudden movement, he stabbed him with a handcrafted dagger he had retrieved from his backpack. Shawn stood still for a few minutes. His eyes were still wet when he joined them.

"He had five deep wounds from the bear's sharp claws. He wouldn't have survived for long. I had to kill him, to put him out of his suffering," he explained.

Leila nodded and hugged him. After a few seconds, he gently pushed her away and said, "We must go. It's not safe here."

Leila then realized these boys had gone through so much that they had partially transitioned into adulthood. They were young men in the bodies of adolescents.

Leila whistled, and Snow and the other dogs came back. They

harnessed them to the sleds in silence and resumed their journey for another two hours to put as much distance between them and their wild encounter as possible. They then stopped to give the dogs some rest, water, and food.

Suddenly, Snow stood up in attention, her head turned, her ears pointed in the direction they had come from, and she snarled. For a moment, Leila feared the bear had followed them. The storm's intensity was decreasing, allowing her to see in the distance what Snow had already perceived: the Jeep was heading toward them. The boys were visibly horrified.

"Art told us that he could find us if we ran away, that the earth was not big enough for us to hide," Michael said.

"Trackers," Leila said. "They must have implanted a tracker in your body at the time of your abduction."

"They are going to kill us. They will not take us back to the facility," Andrew sadly stated.

"We need to keep moving. We should not give up so easily. They're faster than us, but we should be able to get to those rocks before they catch up with us," Michael said, pointing to a rock outcrop that might provide them with some protection.

Shawn pushed the dogs to their maximum speed, and a few minutes later, they took refuge behind the rocks. Leila was not sure that the decision to wait for their opponents was the best approach, but inevitably, sooner or later, they would have reached them. It was probably better to face them than to be shot in the back.

Michael, Shawn, and Andrew took a kneeling position so that the rocks were now protecting them. They hastily removed a fabric bundle from their backpack, placed it at their knee, and unfolded it. To Leila's surprise, the bundle contained handmade slingshots like those used for small animal hunting, steel ammo bullets, modified short metal arrows, and other parts that could be added to the slingshot.

The whole situation was surreal. They were in the middle of nowhere in Alaska, chased by humanoids who intended to kill them, and were fighting back with eighteenth-century weapons. Leila admired Michael, Shawn, and Andrew's bravery and tenacity to fight until the end. However, she wondered what harm such rudimentary weapons could cause to artificial opponents.

Michael looked at her and said, "We trained on targets every night in the house, hoping that a day would come when we would use these weapons against the humanoids."

Her incomprehension and despair must have been reflected on her face.

He explained, "Their operational system is in the front, at the base of their neck. A direct hit will cause a short circuit and deactivate them."

Turning to the others, he added, "Andrew, target the humanoids from the right front seat; Shawn, the left one. I'll take care of one of the two sitting in the back. Then, whoever is ready first will focus on the last one."

Leila closed her eyes for a moment, hoping to control her fear. She telepathically sent Ryan an SOS. When she opened her eyes, the Jeep was stopping about five hundred feet from their position. As the humanoids stepped out of the Jeep, three were hit by an arrow at the crucial point of their necks. Within seconds, their movements became jerky, their knees gave in, and they collapsed like the heap of metal they were. However, before the boys had time to regroup, the fourth remaining humanoid showered the rocks with a hail of bullets.

Shawn was hit above one eye by a ricocheted rock. He started to bleed profusely. Pieces of rock flew everywhere, making it impossible for Michael and Andrew to target the last humanoid.

Undergoing a continuous attack, they lay down, covering their heads with their arms. The boys were frustrated and angry to see their lives threatened by a single humanoid after all they had endured, and this close to freedom.

Thoughts and feelings collided in Leila's head. Above all, there was the nagging question of what could be done to stop this madness. The scenarios were rejected at the speed of light as she was aware that the pieces of rock flying around her were now bigger: the humanoid was getting closer. Then suddenly, the machine gun discharge and bullets hitting the rocks stopped, giving way to an unexpected sound.

They looked at each other, puzzled. Slowly and cautiously, they risked a glance between two rocks. The humanoid was lying on the ground, decapitated, its head a few feet away from them. Further in the air, a remote-controlled perfect miniature replica of a fighter jet was performing a large arc to return toward them.

They left the rocky outcrop, forming a rather peculiar convoy: the Jeep, driven by Leila with Shawn lying down in the backseat, was first; then came the two dog sleds under the control of Michael and Andrew; above them, the miniature jet flew forward and circled back toward them in an endlessly repeated process, showing them the direction to follow.

Less than twenty minutes later, they crossed the path of three giant polar snow crawlers. As soon as they came into view, the lights of the first crawler began to flash like a Christmas tree. The remote-controlled jet landed a few feet behind the last crawler and Leila stopped the Jeep a few steps away from the first crawler. She flew into Alex's arms as he got out.

"Alex, you're my hero. Your jet made it just in time to save our lives," Leila said as she hugged him.

"We were looking for you and stepped in the middle of the action. You had done well on your own. You just needed a finishing touch." Then, looking at the boys, he added, "You're all impressive marksmen. What did you use to deactivate the humanoids?"

"Just some handmade weapons, nothing fancy like this jet. Alex, your beheading with a laser beam from a jet flying at high speed was quite impressive," Andrew said.

Leila let the boys and Alex discuss their respective weapons and skills and turned her attention to Marshal White, who was joining them. She couldn't help but remind him of his attitude when they had first met at the commissioner's office barely nine days ago. "Marshal White, what a surprise to see you here. Did Ryan finally persuade you of what AgroFuture's legal facade was hiding? Or are you here to arrest us for trespassing?"

White looked embarrassed, but Leila did not give him time to answer before adding, "Let me introduce you to my companions. All were abducted when young, enslaved, and forced to work for AgroFuture."

Poked by her sarcasm, White addressed the boys. "I sincerely apologize for our short-sightedness. We never had any reason to suspect AgroFuture; otherwise, we would have acted sooner."

"I was kidnapped five years ago," Michael replied. "Andrew six, Shawn four, and Jason three. Earlier would indeed have been preferable."

"Where's Jason?" Andrew asked.

"At a nearby hospital, and I think that should be our next stop," Ryan replied, looking at Shawn's face and bloodstained parka.

"We'll escort you there, then head to the AgroFuture facility to take possession of the premises while Chief Hilton raids their Anchorage office. I would be grateful to your team if Alex could accompany us since he knows the place's layout," White said.

"More than the layout of the premises, you must worry about

the last humanoid guard in the Control Center. It poses a serious security problem. It will have to be deactivated in person."

"If Ryan is okay with that, I'd love to take care of the deactivation. A little action will do me the most excellent good and warm me up," said Jack.

"You both have the green light. Please take note of everything. We might need such knowledge soon. We'll fly back to Anchorage tomorrow with the boys and await your return there."

CHAPTER 19

Joy and Guilt

December 11

MICHAEL AND ANDREW stayed with Shawn while he was getting a few stitches on his forehead. Ryan and Leila remained in the emergency waiting room. It was a small county hospital but surprisingly quite busy. Leila fought to stay awake even when surrounded by noise and sitting in an uncomfortable chair. She should have been ecstatic and bouncing off the walls—in the past twenty-four hours, they had found and freed four of the missing children and survived a polar bear and humanoid attacks. However, with the stress and the adrenaline rush dissipating, she felt intense exhaustion. She heard Ryan say, "Leila, I'm going out for a few minutes to make a call to update my boss on the present situation." Then, she lost contact with her surroundings.

She didn't know how long she had dozed off but woke up feeling watched. Opening her eyes, she saw Ryan looking at her with tenderness and pride. Realizing she was awake, he hastened to hide his feelings under sarcasm.

"Ah! Did I wake you up? I am sorry. I was wondering if we shouldn't let you rest in this five-star hotel." Then, pointing to

Michael, Andrew, and Shawn, standing behind him, he added, "These three adolescents are dangerously hungry. I'm not sure I can restrain them any longer from ransacking this lovely place in search of food."

Leila stood up, fighting a yawn and trying to shake off the fog messing up her thoughts. She must have looked miserable because they all burst out laughing.

"Of course, now that you're safe, gang up on me," she said, laughing and gazing at the three teens.

They went to a small Italian restaurant highly recommended by the doctor who had treated Shawn. Ryan ordered the eight different twelve-inch thin-crust pizzas listed on the menu.

"Any of them for takeout?" the waitress asked seriously. But, seeing the adolescents now looking at the dessert menu, she added with a smile, "I guessed I shouldn't have asked."

Leila was amazed by the impressive amount of pizza the boys could devour. They ate in silence. Anyone other than her would have thought they were too focused on enjoying their pizzas to waste their time on pointless chatter. Still, she felt they were tormented and could sense the clashing of opposite feelings and uncertainty about expressing them without sounding ungrateful.

Finally, Michael asked, "When are we going home?"

"What would you think if your parents came here instead? You could get reacquainted privately," Ryan replied. Getting no answer, he went on. "Following what happened at AgroFuture, the FBI is closely following the development of the investigation, and Mark, the boss of my division, has contacted the governor of Alaska. While at the hospital, I called him, and he told me that the governor is offering to host you and your family at an undisclosed location, all expenses paid for the next two weeks."

The boys looked at each other without exuberance, still visibly worried.

Andrew asked, "How about the trackers Art inserted in us? If he finds us, he will kill us and our parents."

"Don't worry; we deactivated them for good when we scanned you in the snow crawlers. They will no longer be transmitting. We also had the surgeon remove Jason's while he performed surgery on his arm. If you want, you can also have yours removed when we get to Anchorage tomorrow, so you won't have any more sequels from the past," Ryan said.

They nodded, partly relieved.

"What else is bothering you?" Leila asked them.

They all bowed their heads, visibly ashamed. Then Andrew said barely audibly, "Some of the children still missing are from our village. We don't think we can face their parents."

"Do you know what happened to them? Where they might be?"

"No, we were all brought to AgroFuture to be broken—our determination and individualism destroyed and brainwashed into submission. Once submissive, the children were transferred elsewhere. Most likely in places closer to civilization and not as automated as AgroFuture. We were left behind because they needed a minimum number of enslaved children to operate AgroFuture, and we might not have been as submissive as they would have liked."

"From what we know, there should be seven more children: five girls and two boys," Ryan said.

"Girls only. The two boys tried to escape through the mine tunnels and fell into a shaft. They did not survive."

"How awful. But don't worry—contrary to what you think, your presence will symbolize hope for the girls' parents and closure for the deceased boys' parents," Leila said.

They looked at Leila, processing what she had just told them. Then, realizing her perspective could be accurate, their survivor guilt receded, giving way to anticipation of the happiness to come.

"Thank you," Michael said with a genuine smile.

"It's time to go to bed, kids," Ryan said, trying to avoid a public emotional scene that he felt was looming.

The governor had reserved three adjoining rooms for them in a small hotel. The boys shared the middle room, and Ryan's and Leila's rooms flanked theirs on either side. Guards were also posted outside.

After the boys retired for the night, Leila turned to Ryan and said with a hint of sarcasm, "The governor's offer is not without an ulterior motive, Ryan. This will give the Alaskan authorities time to investigate the AgroFuture case fully before it's disclosed to the public. The governor fears the harassment of journalists and this scandal will paint Alaska in an unfavorable light when this affair comes out. What do the parents think of the offer? Have they been notified already?"

"No, the governor is discussing how to address this with my boss. The governor has proposed that a military team visit the parents, tell them the good news, seize their phones and computers, give them fifteen minutes to pack their suitcases, and escort them to a private airport from where they will be flown to Alaska," Ryan explained.

"My god, such a drastic move, more of a reminder of Gestapo action, quite in contrast with what will most likely be the happiest day of their lives," Leila exclaimed, her voice filled with disbelief.

"Indeed. Mark is exasperated. Politics has reached its limits. Certainly, parents should be notified in person. After all these years, some might faint or even have a heart attack hearing such unexpected news. However, Mark is convinced that they will also want to avoid publicity and will appreciate the governor's offer. So, there is no valid reason for such drastic behavior."

"There is at least one reason for caution. Art and his associates might know by now through AgroFuture Control Center that we have escaped and that their safety is compromised. Then, there is Beth. Fact strongly indicates that she is the mastermind behind the kidnapping, so she is part of this collusion, and she is dangerous and still on the loose."

"Yes, Mark is aware of that. He likes the governor's offer for that one reason. This gives us a two-week reprieve to find Beth and Art before they plan an attack. Eventually, Mark and the governor will most likely reach a compromise—the parents' phones and computers will probably be confiscated, but they will have an hour or two to prepare!"

CHAPTER 20

The Governor's Plan

December 12

THEY ARRIVED AT the small locality airport around ten o'clock the following morning. Jason met them there, coming straight from the hospital. The pilot, Don Maharg, welcomed them aboard the governor's luxurious jet. The mood was light after the well-deserved rest of the night. During the short flight to Anchorage, the boys chatted joyously and told Jason about their fights for survival. Their fears were wiped away, leaving place for glorious adventures that made poor Jason sad about missing it all. To make matters worse, they concluded their story by bragging about the delicious pizzas.

The jet landed in Anchorage and taxied to a section of the airport where a small terminal was reserved for private plane passengers. Apart from a group of six men in black suits, the terminal was empty. One of the men parted from the group and approached them. Ryan stepped in front of them, blocking the man's access to the boys and Leila, forcing him to address him.

The man said with authority, "Sir, we are here by order of Governor Grant. We have been appointed to take care of the children, ensure their safety, and accompany them to an undisclosed location where they will await the arrival of their parents, which is scheduled for tomorrow. As for you and the lady, you will be escorted to a location of your choice."

Ryan's sharp tone surprised Leila. "The children are under my direct supervision. Thus, the location of our choice will be the same as theirs."

"It won't be possible, sir."

"I have no intention of letting you . . ."

Leila stopped listening to the discussion, which suddenly was taking a heated turn. She probed Ryan's mind and felt no frustration or anger at being cavalierly dismissed. For some reason beyond her comprehension, he believed that these men were impostors and that the children were in danger. In arguing, he hoped to buy time to assess the risk of triggering a confrontation with six armed opponents and to plan his intervention accordingly.

Her attention shifted to the other men, and any hope of controlling the minds of at least a few of them to help Ryan was crushed when she realized they were all humanoids. They were standing still, waiting to be instructed on what to do.

The boys had also sensed the gravity of the situation and identified the five still men as humanoids. Acting as if they were bored with what was happening, they pulled back slightly. Out of the corner of her eye, Leila saw them casually drop their backpacks on the floor and kneel to rummage through them. She knew what was to come. It was her clue to act.

"Sir, please," Leila said, stepping forward and touching the arm of the man arguing with Ryan.

As expected, he turned to look at her, annoyed by her gesture and interference. In doing so, the children and Ryan were now partially out of his line of sight. He never saw Ryan's karate move coming straight to his neck and couldn't avoid it. He was knocked out before he could even react. Simultaneously, Leila saw three humanoids being inactivated by an offensive from the boys. Ryan drew his gun and aimed at the fourth humanoid as Leila lowered herself to the ground, grabbing the weapon protruding under the suit jacket of the unconscious man. Using his body to shield herself, Leila shot the fifth humanoid to divert its attention to her and prevent it from targeting the children. A hail of bullets hit her human shield and the top of her shoulder, then silence followed. The boys had reloaded their weapons, and with Ryan, they deactivated the last humanoid.

"Damn," Ryan said, annoyed, looking at her, "you could've been killed."

"I'm fine; I was just craving some attention," Leila replied, pushing the body off her.

"Let me see that shoulder," Ryan replied thoughtfully. "You're lucky; it's barely a scratch. Is everyone okay on your side?" he said, looking at the boys.

"Perfectly fine and happy to have been able to practice our shooting skills again. And to think, we feared our life would become monotonous and boring!" Michael replied.

"What a gang you make," Ryan said, relieved that no one had been hurt. Then, after making sure Leila's human shield was really dead, he said, "Unfortunately, this one won't tell us who hired him. It seems that Alaska is not safe anymore for us now."

"How did you know this man was an impostor?" Leila asked him.

"He didn't identify himself, and neither did he address me by name. He was in a hurry to take charge of the boys. And why the hell do you and I need an escort?"

Ryan picked up his cell phone and called his boss.

"Mark, there was a little welcoming committee consisting of a bunch of scoundrels waiting for us at the terminal in Anchorage. As a result, there is one dead man and five deactivated humanoids. From the faint sound of sirens, the cavalry is coming and will be here soon. Can you make sure we don't get stuck here while they investigate? . . . I don't care what the governor of Alaska wants. There is a spy among his people. The family reunion cannot take place here. . . Mark, I don't trust anyone. Get us on any commercial plane leaving Anchorage within an hour. . . Fine. I'll wait for your instructions."

Leila was feeling unsettled; something was not right. Looking around, she realized that the humanoid at the terminal control desk had never asked for their identity card and port of origin when they entered the terminal and had never reacted during or after the altercation. He had been deactivated. She went behind the counter. An empty terminal was captured on its computer screen. It had been tampered with. Their arrival had not been broadcast live, nor was the violent exchange that had followed. So, who had called the police? Certainly not their attackers. The truth jumped out at her.

"We have to get out of here now," she said forcefully.

"What are you talking about?" Ryan replied. "I will identify myself and explain what happened to the authorities. Mark will confirm my identity, and—"

She interrupted him. She pointed to the screen behind the counter and said, "There is no live transmission; the police are unaware of what happened. All the hubbub we hear is staged. The humanoids must have transmitted what was happening before we deactivated them. Whoever is behind this, hopes we will gently wait for the authorities. The reality is that a band of killers is coming our way."

Leila felt the intensity of Ryan's gaze, his thoughts spinning a hundred miles an hour. The sirens were getting louder. The vehicles were closing in. They were running out of time.

Looking at the boys and her, he shouted, "Race back to the plane; I will join you shortly. I will document the scene before we leave."

The boys reached the plane first. As Leila stepped in, Don asked her, "What's going on? I heard gunshots."

"Prepare for an emergency takeoff. Our lives, including yours, are in danger. We'll be leaving as soon as Ryan gets in. We'll decide later where we will go," Leila replied.

He hesitated, but at that moment, Ryan flew over the stairs and jumped in the plane. Don didn't ask for more information and returned to the cockpit as five cars pulled up in front of the terminal. None had police identification. The plane headed for the runway as Ryan closed and secured its door.

They heard Don inform the control tower, "This is flight Two-one-one-two requesting clearance for takeoff on runway five."

"Two-one-one-two, you are not authorized to take off. I repeat, you are not authorized to take off," replied one of the controllers. "Return to the terminal immediately and submit your flight plan."

"Don't listen to him. I'll back you up," Ryan said, taking the copilot's seat.

"Two-one-one-two , heading for runway five," Don transmitted to the control tower.

A furious order followed his request, but Don ignored it and aimed the jet at the runway. Looking at Ryan, he said, "These guys aren't used to taking orders."

At this point, three bogus police cars pulled onto the runway in pursuit of the jet, to the controller's dismay, who began shouting orders frantically.

"Well, it seems that these guys also forgot to ask permission to use this runway," Ryan said.

One of the speeding cars passed the plane and stopped in the middle of the runway, blocking it.

"They must have a death wish. Hell, we will fly over them. Buckle up, everyone," Don shouted.

The plane accelerated and took off, just a few feet from the car. The two occupants of the vehicle threw themselves out. The jet's wheels narrowly missed them and flattened the car's roof as the plane suddenly rose at an angle of forty-five degrees. The angle and the force of acceleration pinned the plane's occupants to their seats. A broad smile appeared on the boys' faces. They enjoyed the thrilling sensation.

In the cockpit, Ryan released his breath. "It was a close call. I will keep you in mind if I ever need a pilot for a risky operation."

Don smiled, "I will be honored. I was a bush pilot in my youth. The skill doesn't go to waste, and I miss the excitement."

"That's good to know. How far can you take us? We have to go to Washington, DC."

"It's your lucky day; we have the wind in our back. This will allow us to go farther. I can get you up to Montana before we need to refuel."

"I'll let you know where to land," Ryan replied.

Ryan waited for the plane to reach a stable altitude, then left the cockpit to join the others in the passenger cabin. He picked up his cell phone.

"Mark—"

Before he could add anything, Leila heard Mark through the phone yelling angrily, "Ryan, what's going on? I told you to wait for my instructions. Breaking news from the intelligence world indicates that one of my agents has gone rogue, killing five officers, kidnapping four children, and hijacking a plane."

"Mark, it's your lucky day. It could have been worse in terms of public relations. The headlines could have said, *An agent, with the help of a psychic, killed—*"

"I don't appreciate you joking about this. You better have a good explanation."

It took Ryan less than a few minutes to calm Mark down. He sent him the footage he had taken before leaving the small terminal. It proved they were the victims of staging. In the images of the crime scene circulating among the authorities, the body of the commando and the humanoids had been replaced by the bodies of the agents initially sent by the governor. It would take some time for the facts to be investigated and for them to be exonerated of all charges. Meanwhile, it was now impossible to land at a commercial airport—they would be arrested, and the children would be flown back to Alaska.

"Mark, we're heading to Washington, but we'll have to land somewhere in Montana to refuel. What are our options?" Ryan asked.

"I'll find you a private airstrip. Listen to me carefully this time. Stay out of trouble until it's all sorted out. I don't want to hear of any other heroic deeds," Mark ordered.

Mark called back thirty minutes later with further instructions.

PART THREE

CHAPTER 21

Montana, a Land of Opportunity

December 12

"THIS IS NOT what I would call a frequently used airstrip. However, this might play to our advantage," said Don, looking at the short, narrow strip on which the snow had been freshly removed and pushed to its end, forming a respectable snowbank.

"What do you mean by that?" Ryan asked.

"I'll explain later; let me concentrate on this 'opportunity.' Make sure your people are secure while I do a reconnaissance flyover. We might have a rough landing. Close the cockpit door and take a seat in the main cabin. If anything happens, you will be safer there."

Before leaving the cockpit, Ryan briefly looked at the snow-covered ground, the forests, and the mountains before them. The narrow airstrip seemed out of place in this beautiful wilderness.

The boys were playing a game they had found in one of the plane cabinets. Entering the main cabin, Ryan said, "Everyone, get seated, buckle up, and store anything that is not screwed to the floor and could become a flying hazard. We are about to land in the middle of nowhere."

Less than a minute later, the games had disappeared into the luxurious storage cabinets along with their backpacks, and everyone had their seat belts on.

Ryan sat next to Leila and whispered in her ear so the boys wouldn't hear, "Our pilot does not want me in the cockpit. He's worried the landing might be rough."

It was not reassuring, but Leila felt some comfort in having Ryan by her side. The plane started its descent. A few minutes later, the snowbanks could be seen on either side of the jet. The rear wheels touched the ground, but surprisingly, the plane maintained an angle, the nose still pointing up for a relatively long time. When the front wheels finally touched the ground, the plane leveled off for a few minutes, during which Don forcibly braked. Then, suddenly, they heard a loud noise, and the nose of the jet dipped abruptly toward the ground.

Leila closed her eyes, expecting to hear screeching metal noises and the plane careening. But instead, the jet suddenly came to a halt. She looked outside. They were surrounded by snow. The plane was resting in the snowbank at the end of the airstrip. The plane had pushed through it. Don turned the engines off. A moment later, he joined them, smiling.

"Welcome to Montana, a lovely, secluded place full of unforeseen events, one of which I believe has just saved our lives."

"What would that be?" Michael asked.

"The snow. Our encounter with the roof of a car inadvertently parked across the runway in Anchorage damaged our front landing gear. The snowbank provided an ideal cushion for the nose of the plane to land on. Now, let's get out and meet our host."

A minibus was heading toward them, using the land strip as a road. It stopped at the edge of the snowbank. Its driver, a tall man in an inverted fur coat and a cowboy hat hiding his facial features, got out and stood beside the minibus, waiting for them to join him.

Leila paid him no attention; her energy was focused on making her way through the snow in which she was sinking up to the top of her legs. It wasn't until he jokingly said, "Ma'am, you need a little help there?" that she realized his voice was familiar. But his presence in Montana was so unlikely that she stopped all effort to look at him attentively and ensure she wasn't mistaken. He had walked toward them, and she could now distinguish his facial features.

"Robert, is that you?" she asked, astonished.

"Flesh and bones," he said, a broad smile lighting up his face. "Fully enjoying the sight of a dear Texan lady struggling in a few feet of snow!"

"Impossible; the Robert I know would have come immediately to my rescue," Leila replied teasingly.

He laughed, reaching out to lift her in his arms and putting her down on the snow-free airstrip.

"As a member of the Cassidy family, I welcome you to our ranch. And as an FBI agent, I am putting you, Ryan Steele, under arrest," Robert said.

"I'm puzzled. Did Mark mandate you for this job? You see, kidnapping does not fall under your jurisdiction, Robert. Moreover, now that we are on your ranch, this case is too personal for you to get involved with. However, I will keep you informed of any developments," Ryan said seriously, using the exact words Robert had served him a few weeks earlier.

Robert looked dumbfounded for a moment. Then, he replied in a very professional tone, "I don't want to disappoint you, my friend, but you are first accused of murdering several agents. And *that* falls under my jurisdiction."

Then, taking Ryan's hand, Robert pulled him toward him in a hug and said, "I'm glad you made it safely out of Alaska. Please don't hold a grudge against me. From now on, we'll work together to sort out this whole affair."

Ryan returned Robert's hug and said, "Robert, seriously, don't endanger your position by hiding us on your ranch."

"Don't worry; everything's under control. I made a deal with Mark. He is collaborating with our people in Alaska, who are now investigating what happened at the Anchorage airport terminal. Meanwhile, until this is sorted out, you are officially under arrest at an undisclosed location. I happened to be on vacation at the ranch, and the beauty and convenience of our airstrip lured you here."

"I have to say we could have found a worse prison. Let me introduce you to Don, whose piloting skills saved our lives twice, and then to these fine boys I presumably kidnapped," Ryan said.

Robert shook everyone's hand and, pointing at the minibus, said, "Let's go home. Darkness is about to fall. We'll return at dawn tomorrow to get this plane out of sight."

"This first stop is for you, guys. Make yourselves comfortable. There are multiple bedrooms to the left and right of the common area. The beds are made in three of them. The first bedroom on the left is yours, Ryan. Next to it, there is one with bunk beds for the four of you, guys. Don, yours is on the other side, to the far right of the chalet. By the way, Ryan, I left a document in your room. It stipulates that you acknowledge being under arrest and that you surrender to my authority. Please sign it and return it to me tomorrow," Robert said as he stopped in front of a large wooden chalet surrounded by a pine forest.

Ryan gave Robert an intense look, but Robert didn't flinch.

"One more thing, you will find food on the stove for dinner tonight and in the fridge for breakfast tomorrow. I'll pick you up around seven tomorrow morning so you can help with the plane's camouflage."

"What about Leila," asked Michael.

"My mother requested that Leila stay at the main house where there is, and I quote, 'a more suitable room for a lady.' Sorry guys—she said it's 'female privilege.'"

Looking seriously upset, Ryan went straight to his bedroom and slammed the door behind him. As soon as the door closed, his features lost all signs of anger. When Robert mentioned a document to be signed, Ryan knew it was a false request. They had both trained together at the Quantico FBI Academy, and their paths had often crossed. They trusted each other and would have risked their own lives to save the other; there was no need for such a document. Ryan guessed that Robert wanted to convey something important without raising suspicion.

Ryan surveyed the room. The accommodation was spartan: a small wardrobe armoire, a small desk with an uncomfortable chair, a two-drawer bedside table with a nightstand lamp, and a twin-size bed. A brown envelope lay in clear view on the pillow. Ryan broke the seal and extracted a sheet of paper with all the appearance of an official document to be signed. He did not bother reading it. He switched on the nightstand lamp and placed the paper over the cylindrical shade opening. Under the unexpectedly intense light, some letters stood out from the others. He smiled; Robert had used such subterfuge in the past.

He deciphered the message the letters formed when read in a particular order and turned off the lamp. Following the instructions, he lifted a plank off the floorboard under the bed. And there, in a plastic bag, he found a short note and ammunition. Ryan read the note, and his face alternated between surprise and anger. With regret, he concluded that the message did not bode well for the night or the days to come.

There was a stew on the stove. Its aroma filled the air of the common area and was infiltrating the surrounding bedrooms. After a day of starvation, the boys could not resist any longer. They dropped their backpacks in their assigned bedroom and hurried back to the kitchen. They were already eating when Don and Ryan joined them. The food was delicious, and they ate in silence. After dinner, they all sat in the common area, and Don recounted some of his adventures as a bush pilot.

CHAPTER 22

The Cassidy Family Ranch

December 12

LEILA WONDERED WHAT the chalet's interior must look like for Robert's mother to offer her lodging at their house. As the minibus drove them farther down the road, she asked, "Is that chalet usually used for workers?"

"No, the chalet is used in summer to host kids from tough neighborhoods and dysfunctional families. For a few months, they can escape their environment. They help on the ranch, develop new friendships, and learn responsibility. For some, this is the only happy time in their youth worth remembering."

"That's quite a philanthropic gesture."

"Surprised that the family of a tough FBI agent might have some humanitarian leanings?" said Robert with a smile.

Without giving her time to answer, he described the ranch, its history, and its current operation. Then, at a bend of the road, perched on a small hill, the main house appeared—a three-story log house with impressive windows providing a panoramic view of the meadow and mountains, surrounded by majestic pine trees covered with snow caps. Robert stopped the minibus to let her admire the scenery bathing in the diffused sunset light. As the sun set, the Christmas decorations lit up. Leila was momentarily speechless, like Alice discovering Wonderland.

"Robert, this is magnificent."

"Yes, isn't it? This is my refuge when I want to forget the senseless violence of this world."

Leila looked at him, and to her surprise, she sensed his irritation. He didn't give her time to reflect on it more and quickly suppressed his feelings.

"Wait until you see the view from the living room; it's striking."

Robert's parents came to meet Leila as soon as they arrived and welcomed her warmly. They made a lovely couple. Robert's father, Sidney, was a strong and tall African American man whose stature Robert had inherited. However, Robert's mixed racial features came from his mother, who was clearly of South Pacific ethnicity. In her late fifties, Naomi was still beautiful and slim. After a few words of introduction, she took Leila under her wing. Locking her arm in hers, she suggested that the men have a drink while she showed Leila to her room. They were on their way before Leila could even utter a word. You couldn't argue with Naomi.

"Leila, I'm so glad to meet you. Robert told us how special you are. I want to know more about you. But for now, you need some rest. Robert mentioned that you probably don't have any clothes besides what you're wearing now. I put some in your closet. If they don't suit your taste or don't fit you, we can go shopping in town tomorrow," she concluded.

"Thank you, Mrs. Cassidy. This is so kind of you. I am embarrassed to cause you so much trouble," Leila said, hiding her surprise at Robert's attention to such detail. She didn't have time to analyze these facts further.

Naomi added, "No trouble at all. Ah, here's your room. Come down whenever you are ready. Dinner is at six. Also, please call me Naomi."

The room was spacious and welcoming. A look at the walk-in closet left Leila speechless. It was filled with clothes and shoes of her size. Robert must have told his mother of her size, but Leila had never had the impression of being on his radar. She assumed that estimating people's stature came with his professional training.

She found a small container in the bathroom with a handwritten note. *Enjoy a relaxing bath*. She opened it, and the scent of lavender and wildflowers filled the air. She mentally thanked her well-intentioned host. The chalet surely did not match this house's luxury. Female privilege indeed!

Leila made it in time for dinner, fresh and leaving a summer draft in her wake. She was wearing one of the warm sweaters and sexy jeans found in her closet. She saw Robert giving her an appreciative look. His mother glanced at Leila's effect on her son and briefly radiated pride at accomplishing a difficult task.

Dinner was delicious, made entirely of products from the ranch and surrounding farms. Naomi narrated funny and scary encounters with wild animals involving Robert. Leila talked about the bear attack and how the dogs had saved their lives, explicitly highlighting Snow's heroic behavior.

Around nine, Naomi declared she was tired. She advised Sidney to take better care of his health and get early rest. They both left, reinforcing Leila's belief that Naomi had an ulterior motive. She wondered if Robert was aware of his mother's agenda.

He must have guessed her thought, as he said with a tint of

mockery, "It's obvious, isn't it? My mother is actively pursuing a particular agenda. She's a quick judge of character, and she likes you. She's looking for a wife for me, which has proven impossible so far."

"I was just wondering if I was right to think so."

He laughed. "My poor mom. Her timing is wrong for a romantic interlude. Based on my deductions, backed up by disturbing facts, things will get messy tonight. Let me show you what I'm talking about."

Leila followed him to a spacious room that served as an office. Like those in the living room, the panoramic windows overlooked the valley. A giant screen hung on the opposite wall. Robert switched it on, and a bird's eye view of the vast ranch appeared. A multitude of small luminous dots clustered around a location sparkled. He pointed at them.

"We tag our cattle with transmitters so that we can locate them anytime. It's useful when we round them up."

But what caught Leila's attention were a flashing dot and a mark at the end of a darker strip, far distant from the cattle and isolated from each other. Robert waited patiently for her to orient herself on the layout of the ranch. She noticed a structure with a large roof. From there, the roads spread in several directions, but one of the roads connected the flashing dot and the mark to that structure.

"This must be the main house," she said, pointing at the structure. "This must be the airstrip with the mark at its end, and the flashing dot is at the chalet where Ryan, Don, and the boys are staying, isn't it?" she asked excitedly, pointing out each location as she mentioned them.

"Exactly."

"You put a transmitter in the chalet!"

"No. The transmitter was activated not long ago. One in the plane cockpit also started transmitting as the plane circled the airstrip. My men shut it down after we left, and I put a mark over the plane location."

"Oh!" she said, perplexed. "Can the plane transmitter be detected when activated?"

"Yes, it would blink and be noticed by anyone sitting there."

Leila now understood why Don had requested Ryan to return to the main cabin and close the cockpit door. It was not for safety concerns.

"Don was alone in the cockpit when he circled the airstrip, and he closed the cockpit door behind him when he joined us in the main cabin immediately after landing," she explained.

"Don is transmitting your location, so I expect some action overnight."

She sensed in him the same irritation as earlier. This place was his sanctuary of peacefulness, untouched by world violence, and it was about to be defiled by humankind at its worst.

"Does Ryan know who Don really is?"

"I put the information about the plane's transmitter in his room. He must be on his guard by now."

His phone vibrated before Leila could ask him how he planned to thwart an attack when he had no idea what it consisted of. As he picked it up, she focused on the screen, captivated by the chalet's flashing light. What was Don's role in this? They had met him not even a day earlier. In the background, she heard Robert angrily order, "Strike it down."

CHAPTER 23

Shadows in the Night

December 12

DON EXCUSED HIMSELF a few minutes after eight. "The day has been long and exhausting. I'm going to get some rest. I'll see you tomorrow."

"Guys, I am sorry, but I'll follow Don's lead," Ryan said before walking to his room.

"I'm going out to see the stars. Anyone care to join me?" Michael asked.

"There isn't much to do here. I'll go with you," Andrew answered.

"There's a good chance we could see an owl," Shawn said. "Count me in. What about you, Jason?"

"I'll pass. I can't dress properly against the cold with these bandages."

Michael, Andrew, and Shawn set off, enjoying their freedom. The light of the full moon reflected off the snow, giving them enough visibility to see without a flashlight. They walked up to a little hill free of trees to get an unobstructed view of the sky.

While Michael and Andrew gazed at the stars, Shawn, who had always bragged about the acuity of his night vision, focused on their surroundings, hoping to see some representatives of the nocturnal wildlife. When his visual survey reached the partially moonlit chalet, what he saw made his blood run cold.

"What the hell?"

His voice's intonation was so out of place in this peaceful environment that Michael and Andrew looked at him. Shawn pointed at the man getting out of the chalet through Don's bedroom window. Without exchanging words, they ran back toward the chalet.

After resting shortly, Ryan came out of his bedroom just after nine. He intended to be on surveillance for the night. A draft of frigid air from the chalet's other side startled him. He went to investigate. Without knocking, he silently opened Don's bedroom door. A blast of freezing air hit him.

Ryan pushed the door open. The room was bathing in the dim moonlight. Don's bed was unoccupied. A small object sat flashing on the nightstand. Don had just climbed out the entirely opened window. In a split second, Ryan figured out what was happening. He rushed back to the common area and vigorously shook Jason, who was dozing on the sofa.

"Wake up, Jason. Take this gun. Don't hesitate to use it if necessary. We might have some dangerous visitors on their way over. Don is in bed with our enemies. He has transmitted our location and is currently skipping out. I'm going after him."

Grabbing the coat he'd left by the door, Ryan rushed out without further explanation.

Jason looked at the gun Ryan had put in his hand. Nothing he said made sense, but the freezing air filling the room removed any trace of his drowsiness. He hurried, gingerly putting on his coat and boots, and stepped out, heading toward Ryan's voice.

Don had barely sneaked out of the chalet when he heard Ryan say, "Don, are you leaving us so soon? And without even saying goodbye?"

Startled, Don turned slowly toward Ryan, standing a few feet behind him. Partly concealing his right side from Ryan's sight, he retrieved a gun from his jacket. But anticipating his move, Ryan pounced on him before he could aim. Under the force of the impact, Don dropped his weapon and was thrown to the ground, Ryan on top of him. He felt a rock under the snow as his hands touched the ground. He grabbed it and hit Ryan's head. Taking advantage of Ryan's dizziness, he pushed him to the ground. He was about to hit him again when a bullet hit the ground near him. Looking in the direction the shot had come, he saw Jason standing at the edge of the chalet, pointing a gun at him.

"Put the rock down, Don, and get off Ryan. Don't be a fool; I won't hesitate to shoot you," Jason said.

Don emitted an incredulous chuckle. He didn't believe the kid would have the guts or skill to do so. He lunged to grab his gun on the ground. Jason fired, hitting him on his right shoulder. Don screamed in pain, rolling in the snow, closer to his weapon. As he heard footsteps approaching, Jason redirected his aim toward the incoming noise but stopped short of firing at his friends. Seeing Jason distracted, Don reached out for his gun. He was about to grab it when Ryan pulled himself toward him and struck him with a vicious chop to the neck that knocked him to the ground, unconscious. The boys froze momentarily, realizing that Jason might be dead without Ryan's quick intervention. Then, the familiar sound of an approaching drone brought them back to reality.

"Take cover in the woods," Ryan ordered, grabbing Don's gun before joining them.

They soon saw the drone delineating against the starry sky, hitting the roof before Ryan could shoot it down and bursting into flames. Seconds later, an explosion destroyed the entire chalet, sending debris flying in all directions. Protected by the trees, none of them was injured. However, Don was not so lucky. Lying unconscious near the house, he was impaled by a piece of pipe thrown by the force of the explosion.

Leila was lost in her thoughts when she saw the reflection of a fireball on the screen and heard the windows shake. Simultaneously, the flashing light at the chalet's location went out. She turned back to face the windows. Flames rising high in the sky confirmed what the reflection on the screen had let her glimpse.

Robert swore. Still on the phone, he yelled, "The chalet just exploded. That's where the damn drone was going. It was not a surveillance but a suicide drone. Find out who was controlling it. I'll take care of the chalet."

At that instant, Sidney stepped into the room, followed closely by Naomi. He was already on his cell, calling the ranch employees. "Chalet Esperance is on fire. Get everyone there." Then, looking at Robert, he said, "Should they be armed?"

"This is a drone attack. My men are busy figuring out who controlled it. So far, no one has set foot on the property. They would have been detected. Your men are safe to deal with the fire. I'm going to the chalet. Stay here with Mom and Leila."

"I'm going with you. Don't try to stop me, son. *My* ranch is under attack, and one of *my* chalets is on fire."

Ignoring her son and husband, Naomi walked toward Leila.

"Leila, please come with me. We'll let the men take care of this."

As Leila neither answered nor moved, Naomi looked at Robert. "The poor dear is in shock."

Robert approached Leila and put his hands on her shoulders. He turned her tenderly to face him. His gesture brought Leila back.

"Leila, what do you see?" he asked.

She had been frantically reaching out to Ryan and Michael with her mind.

"Everyone is safe, but Don. Debris projected by the explosion killed him."

"Damn. We could have possibly learned a lot from him. Meanwhile, Leila, I would like you to go to the safe room with my mom until we return. I would be reassured if you were there with her."

"Fine, your mother and I will defend the fort and let the knights save the kingdom," Leila replied with a sad smile.

Around midnight, Leila and Naomi saw Sidney drive his truck to the back of the house on the security monitor of the safe room. Sidney and Robert looked exhausted as they stepped inside the kitchen. Their clothes were soiled with ashes and smelled of smoke.

"The fire is extinguished, and I left some men there to ensure it won't reignite from its embers," Sidney said to Naomi. Then, looking at Leila, he added as he was leaving. "Robert will give you more details."

Naomi followed Sidney after wishing them a good night.

Robert briefly told Leila what had happened and concluded, "Ryan and the boys have been relocated to another chalet, where my men will ensure their safety. I have scheduled a meeting tomorrow at eleven in my office. If you don't mind, I would like you to join us. I don't expect any more action for the time being. Now, please excuse me; I seriously need a shower and some rest."

Leila wished him good night and went to her room. She indulged herself with a second hot bath. Incredibly, she fell asleep within minutes of slipping into her bed.

CHAPTER 24

Situation Assessment

December 13

ELEVEN PEOPLE PARTICIPATED in the meeting the following day. Ryan had brought the boys at Leila's request, and Alex and Jack were joining remotely from Alaska. Robert introduced two of his agents: Johanna, a tall, slim, athletic woman with tomboy manners, and Archie, a massive former football player. As soon as they were all seated, Robert opened the meeting.

"I'll start by saying we couldn't find where the drone originated. It was not ground-controlled; it was programmed to act like a homing torpedo, aiming at the emitting signal in the chalet."

"Don's," Ryan said.

"Yes. For this reason, I asked Johanna to gather what we have on Don. Johanna, please take over."

"Our information is still limited, having only recently focused our attention on Don Maharg. So far, we have discovered that he was more than the Alaska governor's private jet pilot; he was married to his daughter. The happy couple was living in the governor's mansion. Governor Grant held him in high esteem, and Don might have influenced some of his decisions. It seems that some laws or at least regulations were bent for AgroFuture. When the story does break out, it will be a very political hot potato, now more than ever. So, it took a while for the governor to come to terms with the facts that Don was involved in the airport and ranch attacks."

"I assume Commissioner Johnston mentioned our AgroFuture inquiry to the governor, who discussed it with Don. We never stood a chance there; our fate had been decided long before we arrived," Alex said.

"The governor categorically denied having informed Don of your suspicions about the company. Commissioner Johnston never mentioned your concern or the meeting with you. He learned about the entire affair after it was confirmed the children had been detained at AgroFuture."

"Impossible. Don knew who we were. He must also have been in cahoots with the thugs waiting for us at the terminal," Ryan added.

"We believe the governor was not the leak. We discovered that, years ago, when Don was a freelance pilot, he flew the governor's close and extended family several times to wildlife refuges in Alaska. He had an affair with the governor's younger sister, who is now known as Commissioner Johnston. This is also how he met the governor's daughter, who he later married. We believe the Johnston-Maharg affair survived both lovers' marriages and never ended. If this is true, Commissioner Johnston is the leak. She is being questioned as we speak."

"Wow, this qualifies as a 'family affair,'" Alex joked.

"Why did Don help us escape, flying us out of Anchorage, and not hand us over to his henchmen if he wanted us dead?" Leila asked.

"I think he was surprised by how quickly the events escalated," Robert replied. "No one expected such resistance on your part. So, when you all returned to the plane requesting him to take off, he believed that doing otherwise would jeopardize his cover. In any case, he was outnumbered and would have lost a fight. So, he reacted appropriately, knowing he had other tricks up his sleeve.

"He suggested landing in Montana to refuel. He knew he would have help eliminating us here," Ryan said.

"What was his role in AgroFuture's business?" Leila asked.

"We still don't know. This is one of the loose ends we are currently investigating," Johanna answered. "Maharg was an exemplary citizen. His name is not in any of our criminal databanks. We collected his fingerprints and are presently running them. They haven't turned up on anything yet."

"I don't believe people turn criminal overnight," Robert said. "He wouldn't have hesitated to kill any of you last night. He was an informant for AgroFuture, to say the least, which could have resulted in your death at the facility, airport, and chalet. He must have a criminal record. We only need to find it."

"It will be interesting to see what you find," Ryan said. "He was probably one of the top decision-makers at AgroFuture. No bullets were ever fired at the plane. His thugs only try to stop us from taking off. Don took pleasure in teaching them a lesson, scaring them, and showing them how stupid they were and how mad he was at them. He was a daredevil."

"What about the AgroFuture office in Anchorage? Any clues there?" Leila asked.

"Completely wiped out—not even a paperclip left behind," Archie replied. "The money has evaporated also. The bank account never had much money; any profit was constantly rerouted. We're looking into it."

"What about you, Alex?" Robert asked. "Did you find anything that could help us at the facility?"

"No, Art did a good job there, too. We only found an old, damaged photo taken fifty or sixty years ago. It probably slipped out of a wallet without its owner's knowledge. It was stuck in the wall trim behind a dresser. I was able to restore part of it. This is the original."

A faded and discolored photo appeared on the wall screen. A young couple stood on either side of a tree where a heart had been carved into the bark. Their heads leaned on the tree, and their hands framed the carved heart. It was impossible to make out the words engraved in the heart, the photo being out of focus. Over half of the man's face was also missing, resulting from a tear.

"I focused on the woman," Alex said. "The man will require much more work since I must reconstruct most of his features."

The woman's retouched and enlarged face appeared on the screen. The image was still grainy and less focused than they had hoped, but it was much better than the original. It nevertheless provoked a reaction from the boys, who whispered to each other.

"She must have been nineteen or twenty in this picture. I noticed a certain resemblance to our sketches of Beth. I also did an age progression," Alex said.

A series of computerized sketches filled the screen.

"Hold on, Alex," Leila said. Then, looking at the boys he asked, "Who is she?"

Her question was met with silence and a visible attempt to avoid her gaze. The atmosphere grew thick with tension. Then, finally, Shawn said sadly, "Someone looking a lot like her was bringing the children to AgroFuture, coming back to pick them up when they were broken. But she wasn't in her sixties or seventies, like this one would be now."

"So, this woman resembles Beth but cannot be Beth. The photo was taken too long ago. However, Beth can be her daughter and could have lost the photo while visiting AgroFuture. This would corroborate Beth's involvement in child abduction, enslavement, and her association with AgroFuture," Leila concluded.

"Beth did not seem to be directly implicated in AgroFuture. However, if you remember, the commissioner said that AgroFuture was expanding its business beyond Alaska. What if she wasn't talking about its market but about another facility? Alex, do you have a list of companies specializing in hydroponic culture?" Ryan inquired.

"I have programmed a search but haven't had time to look at the result yet. Give me a second. Ah! Here is the list." Alex froze. "Oh my god."

"What?" they all said in unison.

CHAPTER 25

Danny, Beth's Protégé

December 13

D ANNY WAS LOST in his thoughts. In front of him was a plate with the toast and scrambled eggs—now cold—that he had cooked for breakfast. In his twenties, he was proud of his accomplishments. However, the events of the past few months and, more specifically, Beth's behavior over the past few days had left him perplexed.

He had great respect for Beth. She had saved him from prostitution when, at the age of sixteen, he had been kicked out on the street by his parents, who were addicted to opioids and no longer wanted the burden of an adolescent who, in their mind, was old enough to support himself. Beth had acted like a caring mentor, almost like a mother at times.

He didn't know much about her personal life besides what she had told him: she had inherited a substantial sum of money and wanted to use it to save humanity from starvation. She had bought a large property consisting mainly of a small house and a mountain with a large underground limestone cave. She had built a larger home for herself, and Danny had remained in the original house.

They had transformed the cave into a hydroponic farm and started operating on a small scale. She took care of the finances, he oversaw the day-to-day operations, and together, they discussed expansion and the future direction of the business. She was rarely on location and trusted him completely.

With each stage of expansion that required staffing, Beth had brought one or two teenage girls who, she explained, had committed serious criminal offenses. A judge had agreed to commute their jail sentence into a work sentence in a company with a humanitarian goal on the condition that they be isolated from society. Any contact with the outside world, even with their parents or close relatives, was forbidden. Their education was basic, and Beth had no obligation to improve their condition. She had asked him to be tough on them so they would understand that hard work was their survival insurance.

Danny was not comfortable in this situation. It reminded him of his past life. He would have much preferred to deal with employees. He had expected the girls to be rebellious and wild, but strangely, they were submissive; all resistance seemed to have been drained out of them. They never spoke to him, conforming to the code of silence they had established for themselves. Regardless, he had pitied them and brought them on excursions in the mountain a few times when Beth wasn't there.

Beth used to come back to the facility once or twice during the year and never stayed more than a few weeks each time. During these visits, she seemed pleased to be back, enjoying long walks and going to the nearby town for shopping sprees. She had returned in August this time, and unlike her usual visit, she looked preoccupied. She had not set foot outside the property's perimeter for nearly five months and had shown no intention of leaving.

He couldn't explain her behavior toward the girls either: she openly hated them. He had to convince her that the girls should spend some time outside the cave, getting sun and fresh air to avoid getting sick.

Nevertheless, she argued, "Fine, make them work longer in the evening and let them go out half an hour in the interior court during the day to get some sun and fresh air. They are indispensable to maintaining our production. They are our workforce for the coming years, so they will have to redouble their efforts if we are to expand further."

Then, catching his concerned look, she added, laughing, "You have a soft heart, Danny. Don't worry; I'll whip them myself from now on."

He had never seen this dark side in Beth before, and while he wondered what the future held for them, two men and a woman had arrived unexpectedly a few days ago. Without further introduction, Beth had locked herself with them in her office.

The visitors never left; Beth hosted them in her house. With their arrival, events escalated even further. Beth became distant, cold, and bossy with him. He wondered if she had not decided to sell the business without letting him know and if he wasn't about to lose what he had worked so hard for.

"I can assure you that this will end soon, Beth. I plan to eliminate these agents once and for all, especially Leila and Ryan. They will not destroy what I have built without consequences. I'll keep you posted on any developments and decisions I'll make concerning the future of our organization. If it comes down to it, we can always rebuild what we have in another country."

This conversation had occurred ten days earlier when Beth's mentor and leader had informed her of the events unfolding in Alaska. Beth didn't understand how the agents had found out about AgroFuture, but she was persuaded that it was related to their relentless quest for her. She profoundly hated them, and their deaths would bring her intense joy.

Years earlier, she had been involved in the Alaska and Montana business start-ups. She was going to these facilities when the fools in Vermont thought she was neurasthenic and needed to be institutionalized. Those poor idiots had no idea their own children were working as enslaved people in their businesses. It was her revenge for those who had caused the loss of her child and crushed all her hopes of motherhood. This summer, she had narrowly escaped the manhunt to find her and made it undetected to Montana. More than ever, Montana was her haven.

But, after losing AgroFuture, she was now at risk of losing her Montana retreat, thanks to Art, who did not have the guts to kill the agents before leaving AgroFuture. He had left it to nature and the humanoids to perform the task assigned to him. The agents had survived and had become a threat to her.

She despised Art deeply. She had been waiting all night for him to return from his last assignment, and she was on edge and exhausted. Then suddenly, without even knocking, Art and his two accomplices burst into her office.

"The drone did its job. We heard the explosion and saw the flames rising from where we were," Art said confidently.

"The issue at stake is: do you know if the agents and the boys were killed?" she asked.

"Well, the drone targeted the signal that Don had set up. This is where they should have been, as he mentioned when he texted us before landing. So, we can assume that they are dead."

"*Assumed* is not proof of success. Where's Don?"

"He never showed up at the rendezvous point. We waited for him all night. We couldn't stay there any longer without risking being discovered, so we left."

"You see, Art, the problem with you is that the job is always half done and ends up a failure."

"What else could we have done? We couldn't go to the ranch and ask them if the agents and the boys were dead!"

Beth didn't answer, but if he had failed again to eliminate those threatening her existence, she intended to kill him. Now, she needed to know what was happening at the ranch and what had happened to Don.

She called Danny and asked him to join them.

"I have just been informed that there was a fire at the Cassidy ranch last night. The ranch is one of our good customers. Gather some of today's fresh products and deliver them yourself. Help them if necessary. When you return, let me know if the fire resulted in much damage and if anyone was hurt," she immediately said as he entered the room.

Her demeanor and authoritarian tone indicated that she intended to be obeyed without being questioned. She had no intention of telling him how that news had reached her. He assumed her "guests" must have gone into town earlier this morning and heard about the fire. He had just seen them coming back. He looked at them, but they ignored him. He was just a subordinate, a fly on the wall.

Beth's tone brought him back to reality.

"Danny, get moving," she barked.

CHAPTER 26

A Harsh Reality

December 13

BEFORE ALEX COULD answer, Robert's phone rang.

"Hold on, Alex. I need to take this call." Turning his speaker on, he said, "Lee, what's going on?"

"A man driving a delivery van just showed up at the gates, and Mrs. Cassidy buzzed him through. He is driving toward the main house as we speak."

"Any business ID on the van?"

"The lettering read *The Enchanted Spring*."

"That's the hydroponic company I was about to tell you. It's located near the ranch," Alex exclaimed.

Leila repeated pensively, "The Enchanted Spring!" She looked at Ryan. "This can't be a coincidence."

"I don't believe in coincidence either. I think we found out where Beth is hiding. She is most probably the drone owner," Ryan concluded.

"If you're right, she might have sent this guy to get an update, learn if the operation was successful, and what happened to Don, whose death was certainly not part of the plan," Robert said.

"This can be played both ways: I can learn much more from him than he can suspect," Leila said.

"Tread carefully, Leila. This guy might be dangerous," Robert said.

When Leila reached the kitchen, the delivery man was already there. She heard Naomi saying, "Danny, it's so nice of you to bring us all these fresh fruits and vegetables."

"It's nothing, just a small gift from Beth. When I learned there was a fire at the ranch, I feared for you and your husband. What exactly happened?" Danny replied.

Before Naomi could answer, Leila made her entrance.

"I'm sorry to interrupt you. I'll get something to eat and be on my way." Leila smiled, but seeing the fresh fruits Naomi was pulling out of the delivery box, she exclaimed, "Oh, these fruits look so fresh. They smell so good. It's as if they were just picked this morning."

"We did indeed just pick them," Danny answered.

"Danny, let me introduce you to Leila. She is my son's girlfriend," Naomi said with a sly smile and a look daring Leila to contradict her. Then, as if she knew Leila's intent, she added, "Danny is the manager of The Enchanted Spring, a local company doing hydroponic culture. He has been our supplier to the ranch for several years already, and we have become quite acquainted. He's a trusted friend."

Leila gently touched Naomi's shoulder to reassure her, and looking at Danny, she said, "I didn't know Montana had hydroponic agriculture. Where is your farm located?"

"Inside a limestone cave in the mountain. We adapted it, allowing us to cultivate in a controlled environment yearlong without interruption."

"I would love to visit your facilities," Leila said enthusiastically.

"I'm sorry. Beth, the owner of the facility, would not allow it."

"We'll keep it our secret."

"Impossible; she lives on-site, as we all do."

"You also have employees?"

"A few," he answered elusively.

Leila's questions made Danny uncomfortable. However, they allowed her to capture the images they aroused in his mind: two houses near the mountain's entrance, a cave with a controlled environment, and five young girls picking berries. She recognized the kidnapped girls from the children's sketches.

Looking at Naomi, he tried changing the subject of the conversation. "Can I be of any help cleaning up the mess from the fire?"

Leila sensed it was time for her to go on the offensive.

"I'm afraid it won't be possible," she replied before Naomi could answer him. "The crime scene is under investigation."

"The crime scene? An investigation? What happened? Have people been hurt?" He seemed honestly surprised.

"The fire was set intentionally by someone to cause the death of several guests. I must admit this is quite unbelievable in such a peaceful and beautiful place," Leila paused, looking at Danny intensely. She could only sense surprise and disbelief in him.

In an innocent and nonthreatening tone, she added, "How did you learn about the fire?"

"Beth asked me to check on you, bring you some fresh produce, and offer my help," he said, looking at Naomi.

And there it was: Leila saw, in his mind, the meeting he had this morning with a woman looking like some of the sketches they had of Beth and the woman in Alex's old photo, confirming that she was their wanted fugitive. In addition to Beth, Art and the couple in charge of the Anchorage AgroFuture office were also present at that meeting, confirming the assumption that AgroFuture and The Enchanted Spring were part of the same organization. As suspected, Beth was the common link to both.

Naomi and Danny were looking at Leila. Naomi had suspected straight from the beginning that Leila had been sent to question Danny, who, for a reason she ignored, was suspected of being the arsonist.

Danny gradually doubted Leila's innocent act; after all, she seemed to be the girlfriend of Naomi's son, an FBI agent, and he wondered where she was going with her inquiry. The truth suddenly dawned on him. "Naomi, I swear I had nothing to do with the fire," Danny said in a desperate tone, pleading with Naomi to believe him.

"I know, Danny. Don't worry, Leila didn't mean that. Am I right, Leila?" Naomi replied emphatically.

Leila smiled to reassure them and said, "Not anymore, but I believe others at The Enchanted Spring are responsible for it."

Danny's shock and then disbelief reflected on his face. Thoughts swirled in his head. He processed the full intent of what Leila had said, and after a few minutes, he asked, "What do you mean by that?"

"Let me introduce you to the people targeted by the attack."

Leila introduced Danny to the group, and they briefed him on AgroFuture, Art, Don, last night's fire, and the children's kidnappings.

"Danny, can you look at these sketches of the kidnapped young girls and confirm that they are the girls currently working at The Enchanted Spring?" Robert asked.

They all saw the surprise on Danny's face as he recognized the girls.

"Yes, it's them, but Beth couldn't have played an active role in their abduction. She showed me the court orders, signed by the judge, authorizing her to be the girls' guardian. She can't be a kidnapper, let alone a cold-blooded killer. Art and the other couple must have forced her to do what they wanted. They're likely the ones who attacked you last night. They're probably in cahoots with your dead guy," he said, trying to defend Beth.

He was visibly conflicted. Although he had a filial attachment to Beth, he couldn't deny the coldness of her personality, which he had seen grow more intense over the last few months.

In a final attempt to convince him of Beth's active involvement, Leila asked Alex to project the photo he had found at AgroFuture.

"Danny, have you ever seen this photo, or do you know who these people are?"

"How did you get this photo? I have seen it in Beth's wallet. Based on her attachment to this photo and her resemblance to the woman, I assumed these were her parents when they were young."

"The photo was found behind a dresser in one of AgroFuture's guest rooms. According to Jason, Andrew, Shawn, and Michael, a woman looking a lot like this woman was bringing the girls to AgroFuture's Alaska location to be broken and was coming back to pick them up when ready," Leila said.

It was as if the ground had split open beneath Danny's feet. The reality of who Beth was shocked him, and the fact that he had unwillingly and reluctantly participated in an enslavement ring slowly dawned on him. He was horrified. "Oh, my god. What have I done? I believed her, helped her keep these girls, and made them work like slaves. I didn't know. The girls never spoke to me," he said, choking.

Staggered, he got up and walked over to the window, looking toward the mountains where he knew Beth was anxiously waiting for him to report in. The silence dragged on for a while, broken only by his sobbing. Naomi got up to comfort him. When he finally turned back, he had regained his composure, but his eyes were still glassy and his voice quivered.

"What do you expect from me?" he said, clearing his throat.

"We need your help to break up this gang and rescue the girls.

We must know how to access the facility and what to expect there."

They used the next hour to familiarize themselves with The Enchanted Spring and elaborate a plan to storm the facility, which included some time for Danny to hide with the girls in a safe location until the operation was complete.

CHAPTER 27

The Enchanted Spring Facility

December 13

"WHAT TOOK YOU so long?" Beth snarled when Danny stepped into her office.

"I went to the ranch and to town afterward for some errands. Naomi is sending her regards; she was grateful for the gift," Danny answered.

"Did you learn anything valuable concerning the fire?" Art asked.

"An explosion in a chalet resulted in the death of seven guests, four adolescents and three adults. The location is off-limits and under investigation. Sounds awful," Danny answered, staring at Art before turning around and leaving.

"Three adults! Do you believe him?" Art asked as soon as Danny exited the room.

"He has no reason to lie. Moreover, this would explain why Don never showed up at the rendezvous point and hasn't contacted us since then. He activated the tracker but couldn't leave the chalet before the scheduled attack. I guess we'll never know what exactly happened there."

"But the fact remains that he was killed in the blast, and this is bad news, even though the intended targets were successfully eliminated," Art said, completing Beth's thoughts.

"Yes, more than you can imagine," Beth said, picking up her cell phone.

Looking at Art, she wondered if she shouldn't kill him now and be proactive since Don's death had undoubtedly sealed his fate. It would prove that she had nothing to do with his incompetence. Art could easily follow Beth's silent reasoning. He knew exactly where he stood now. He had no intention of staying any longer.

Danny had just left the house when he heard gunshots. It surprised him. He hadn't expected events to escalate so quickly and take such a turn. One thing was for sure: he didn't want to face whoever had survived the shooting.

It was now impossible to follow the plan elaborated earlier at the ranch; he had to improvise. He sprinted toward the tunnel entrance leading to the large cave where the girls would all be working at this hour.

As soon as the door of the large cave slid back, Danny destroyed the operating panel that controlled its operation, locking the door into a closed state. He turned around. The five girls had stopped working and were staring at him, eyes wide open, visibly worried: they were trapped in the cave until the panel could be restored.

"Grab your water and the fruits and vegetables you have already picked, and follow me," he ordered without explaining.

They ran to a small adjacent storage cave at the far end of the main cave. Once inside, he ordered, "Help me move the boxes stacked on this back wall. Use them and anything here to block access to this cave."

As the boxes were moved, a sliding door panel and, on the ground, a small flat stone, previously concealed, came into view. Danny lifted the stone, and a control panel popped up. He punched in a code, and the door panel slid open. Except for a small perimeter illuminated by the storage cave's light, total darkness was beyond it.

In the early days of the central cave transformation, Danny had installed the sliding door panel to ensure stable control of the agricultural environment in the large cave. However, he had yet to seal the opening permanently, thinking of a possible future expansion.

Danny pushed the control panel back to its original position and placed the small rock over it. He then opened the emergency kits he had snatched at the mountain and at the large cave entrances and gestured to the girls to join him.

"Put these on," he said, distributing some headlamps from the kits. He switched his headlamp on and illuminated the dark interior of the tunnel.

"This tunnel is connected to another large cave. When you reach the cave, walk along the wall to your right. You will find another tunnel halfway. Wait for me there."

"You're not coming with us?" one of the girls asked.

He looked at each of them. They were visibly frightened, enough to break their established code of silence. They had always obeyed his orders without a word, and he had grown accustomed to this type of relationship. But this was not an ordinary situation. When he answered, his voice had lost its authoritarian tone.

"Not right now. I have a few details to take care of to ensure our safety."

He was suddenly interrupted by the sound of loud bangs on the door of the main cave. The girls jumped and grabbed each other's arms, looking at him desperately.

"If I don't show up, move on without me," he added swiftly, more than ever pressured by time. "Several tunnels will intercept one after another. *Only* follow the tunnel with a small white mark at the junction of the wall and floor," he emphasized before adding, "You will eventually reach a large cave with a water pool and a small water cascade at one extremity. Help will come within a few days at most. Now, go, go."

He had explored the network of tunnels and caves. It was a maze, a dangerous, treacherous underworld with unexpected hazards. Finding this last cave had taken him several cautious explorations. If his attempt to stop their pursuers failed, then the network of tunnels and caves and all its dangers could act as a backup and thwart their rushed attempt to find the girls.

He ran to the opposite wall of the small cave, where he grabbed a wooden box from an upper shelf. He stepped inside the tunnel and, staying within the perimeter of the diffusing light, assembled the explosives contained in the box he had just retrieved. He was working fast, conscious that, due to a lack of time, he was not accurately estimating the force of the explosion.

Suddenly, he heard several gunshots, and the glass door shattered.

"Danny, where are you?" Art yelled. "Beth sent me to tell you she intends to start a new venture elsewhere, for which you will oversee the operations. She will leave in the next hour and wants you to accompany her. Let me help you pack the essentials."

Danny didn't even ponder the offer. He didn't know what had happened at the house earlier and wasn't sure if Beth was still alive. But after learning who these people were, he could trust neither Beth nor Art. They did not intend to leave any witnesses or traces of their presence here, and his fate and that of the girls was sealed.

He could clearly distinguish the fast-moving footsteps of at least two people going row by row in the main cave looking for them. He had only a few minutes left before Art and his companion would reach the small cave. He pushed a small button on the control panel affixed to the rock next to the opening on the tunnel side. The panel door slid into place. He stepped into the darkness, hoping to be far enough away to survive the blast.

———·———

The boxes blocking the small cave entrance were now being pushed out. The top ones tumbled down under the efforts of Art and his companion. Stepping into the small cave, they heard the faint noise of the panel door sliding back into place. Art smiled.

"Poor Danny. Do you think this would stop us?" Art said loudly and disdainfully.

No interrupter being apparent, Art blasted the panel door with a volley of bullets and kicked what was left down. In the distance, they saw Danny's dancing light receding into the darkness.

"Go after him," Art ordered his companion.

"It's pitch dark in there."

"Follow his light; I'll be right behind you."

As his companion stepped inside the tunnel, Art heard a faint click. His instinct warned him of danger, and he threw himself back as the tunnel exploded.

———·———

Art lay motionless on the small storage cave floor. He could feel his heart pounding. He had lost his hearing. The air was heavy, filled with dust. He swore. Danny must have installed a dead man switch; seeing it in the dark was impossible, and his companion must have unknowingly triggered the mechanism. As the dust settled down, he saw a pile of rocks totally obstructing the tunnel and, barely visible, his companion's feet, the rest of his body crushed under the rocks. More than ever, he wanted to kill Danny.

The force of the blast projected Danny forward as he ran through the tunnel. He hit his head hard on a rock protruding from the wall. An intense pain jolted his brain, followed by dizziness and nausea. He fell. He thought of Leila. She had told him earlier that she was a telepath, that she would perceive his distress signal if he was in a desperate situation. He highly doubted the accuracy of such a statement, but he hoped nevertheless she would perceive his desperate call for help. She was now their only chance of survival. A wall of blackness fell over him, and he lost consciousness.

After Danny's departure, Robert summoned all his team to his office, and Naomi went to the kitchen to prepare food for her "gladiators." She returned to the office with a cart full of fresh homemade bread, some produce from the ranch, including lunch meat and honey, and the fruits and vegetables Danny had brought earlier.

The discussion focused mainly on what had been learned about The Enchanted Spring facility, including the best way to storm it while minimizing the risk of being injured or killed, and capturing Beth and her guests alive. Leila did not participate actively in the discussion. She was distracted most of the time.

Before adjourning the meeting, Robert summarized the operation in detail and the role each would play. He concluded by saying, "Leila, you'll stay at the ranch with the guys," designating Michael, Andrew, Shawn, and Jason. "We'll keep in touch," he added teasingly, indicating his cell phone. "Everyone, Operation Beth will start tomorrow at dawn."

The team left, but Leila didn't move. She had felt a growing uneasiness during the meeting. She had pushed it aside, believing she was projecting what Danny must be feeling: tremendous stress and fear of what would happen the next day. In fact, without realizing it, she was in direct contact with Danny's emotions. The feelings intensified when Danny blew up the tunnel entrance, culminating with his last cry for help before passing out.

Leila was then hit by severe pain in her head and over her entire body. She felt dizzy. She moaned. Then, emptiness and darkness followed. She heard Robert and Ryan call her name several times in a daze. Light pressure on her arm brought her back to reality. She took a deep breath, searching for air like a drowning survivor.

"Leila, what just happened?" Ryan asked, visibly concerned by her strange behavior.

"Danny, the girls. Art is trying to kill them," she said. "We cannot wait; we must go there now. Tomorrow will be too late."

CHAPTER 28

The Cave

December 13

AS DANNY HAD mentioned, the tunnel led to another cave. Following his instructions, the girls found the entrance of the next tunnel. They were waiting for him to join them when they heard the explosion. Their headlamps lit up a cloud of dust coming out of the tunnel they had exited a few minutes before. Stunned, they tried to process what was going on. When Danny did not come out of the tunnel, reality sank in.

"We are trapped. Danny sealed our exit out and left us here to die," Shelby said. At twelve, she was the youngest of the group.

"Don't be stupid, Shelby. He would have left us in the hydroponic cave to be killed if he had wanted us dead. He saved our lives by coming back and showing us where to hide," Caitlin, the tallest of the group, answered.

"Caitlin is right. We must go back and see if he's hurt," said Rihanna, who always sided with Caitlin and was her best friend.

"No, it's too dangerous. He told us to go on without him if he didn't show up," Sarah argued. She was barely a few months older than Shelby and felt a sisterly attachment to her.

"Stop arguing," Arianna, the oldest of the group, ordered. "Caitlin and Rihanna, go back to see what happened to him. We'll wait for you here."

Arianna wasn't the tallest or fittest, but she had established her authority long ago, and messing with her had severe consequences. So, without further arguing, Caitlin and Rihanna returned to the cave and cautiously walked back into the tunnel leading to the storage cave. They had barely walked a third length of the tunnel when they found Danny unconscious, face down. Caitlin knelt by his side and gently shook his shoulder.

"Danny, can you hear me?" Receiving no answer, she addressed Rihanna. "Help me turn him on his back. Hold on; I'll first secure his head."

Caitlin took off her apron, folded it, and placed it slightly under Danny's head to protect it from the bare rocks. Danny's body was quite heavy for them, but they succeeded in rolling him on his back.

"His headlamp is crushed, and he has a huge bloody bump underneath. I don't see any injuries other than a few superficial scratches on his face," Caitlin noticed.

Hearing noises deeper into the tunnel, they both looked in that direction. Rocks still fell at intervals; the ceiling and walls were unstable and crumbling.

"We have to get out of here. It's not safe. The whole tunnel may soon collapse on us," Rihanna said.

"We can't leave him here. He'll be crushed," Caitlin answered, concerned.

"How are we going to transport him? He's too heavy for us to lift. Even then, we couldn't share his weight on our shoulders. We don't have a stretcher either."

Caitlin looked around, and her gaze lingered on Rihanna's thick denim apron. It was like hers, but since it was too long, Rihanna had folded it up to her waist, brought the apron ties around her waist, and tied a knot in the front over the fold to keep it in place. This gave her an idea.

"Take off your apron and give it to me. Get the others; we will need them. Hurry up, and don't let Arianna bully you out of it."

Rihanna sprinted out, relieved to leave the tunnel. Caitlin looked around; darkness surrounded them, the rocks still crumbled in the background. Fear crept into her. To reassure herself, she decided to talk to Danny. Whether he could hear her or not did not matter. His presence, the presence of another human being with whom she could communicate, was comforting. She gently removed her apron from under Danny's head and replaced it with a flat rock.

"Sorry, Danny, it will be slightly uncomfortable, but only for a few minutes."

The noise at the end of the tunnel intensified. It might have been her mind playing a trick on her, or another section of the ceiling had just collapsed. They were running out of time.

"Hang on, Danny. We're going to get you out of here."

She tied both aprons together as tight as she could using their neckties and laid the cloth alongside Danny. Suddenly, the other end of the tunnel came alive. Caitlin counted four headlamps and distinguished four silhouettes of different sizes. Rihanna had convinced them to come and help her. Rihanna reached her first; the others hesitantly followed her.

Rihanna whispered to Caitlin, "Sorry it took so long; I had to threaten Arianna that she would face a mutiny if she didn't come. She didn't cooperate in good faith."

Caitlin smiled. She was relieved. Together, they could carry Danny out of this dangerous place. Arianna's willingness was the least of her concerns.

"Don't worry, I will handle her," she said in a tone barely audible to Rihanna.

Then, addressing the group, now reaching them, she said, "Arianna, as you mentioned earlier, saving Danny's life is a priority for our survival. You made a wise decision."

Arianna, who didn't expect to be praised for a decision she hadn't even considered, was too imbued in herself to believe that Caitlin was manipulating her. So, in a condescending tone, she answered, "What do you have in mind?"

"We'll slide the aprons under him. We can then secure the apron ties around his body to hold him firmly, making a kind of stretcher. We can use the edges of the aprons to lift and carry him."

Arianna took a moment to visualize what Caitlin had imagined and nodded.

"I will lift him by the shoulders; you and Rihanna take his legs. Sarah and Shelby, be ready to slide the aprons under him as far as you can," Arianna ordered, taking charge of the operation.

After several efforts, they finally secured Danny's body and carried him out of the tunnel. They went on until they reached the entrance of the second tunnel. Exhausted, they put him down on the ground.

"We'll never be able to carry him plus the food and water," Shelby complained.

"No, we'll leave him here, find the other cave, and return later to carry him," Arianna decided. But seeing Caitlin's disapproval on her face, she promptly added, "Caitlin can stay with him."

As they left, Rihanna whispered to Caitlin, "You should be safe here. I will come back as soon as I can."

"Don't worry. We'll be fine. Thank you."

"Rihanna, we're waiting for you. Hurry, we have to get going," Arianna ordered.

The girls went farther into the tunnel. Their progression was slow; they had to circumvent or climb rocks that obstructed the tunnel in several places. They finally reached a small chamber. They stood there for a moment, looking around. They faced three breaks in the wall, indicating the entrance of three other tunnels. From where they stood, they couldn't see any marks that indicated the direction to take.

"There're no marks," Sarah said, exhausted and disappointed.

"Danny said that the marks were located at the junction of the wall and floor. It's too dark to see them from here," Arianna said.

They split up to scrutinize the entrance of each tunnel more closely.

"I can see something small and white here," Shelby said.

They gathered around her.

"That must be it," Arianna said.

"There is a similar mark at the tunnel entrance we just left. We will be able to retrace our path," Rihanna confirmed.

They encountered two more intersections, repeating the same exercise each time. They were halfway through the fourth tunnel when it got so narrow that even Shelby and Sarah couldn't go through side by side. They stopped, unsure if they should continue.

Arianna ordered, "Shelby, go ahead; you're the smallest. See if the tunnel leads somewhere."

"Send Rihanna; she's taller and larger than me. If she can go through, so can we."

"You're just scared and don't want to admit it. If Danny went through it, any of us should be able to," Rihanna said before going on her own.

They heard her footsteps echoing in the dark, and suddenly, a short scream, then silence filled the void. They looked at each other, their anxiety growing with every passing minute.

"Rihanna, can you hear me? What's happening? Are you all right?" Arianna called.

Her voice echoed in the tunnel, but Rihanna didn't answer.

Caitlin tore and ripped the lower part of her relatively clean T-shirt in half. She wet both pieces with the water she had kept. She moistened Danny's lips with one and cleaned his wound with the other. He moaned. She removed her headlamp and placed it on a nearby rock to avoid blinding him when he regained consciousness.

"Danny, please wake up," she said softly, taking one of his hands into hers.

She felt his fingers move, and he slightly squeezed her hand. She touched his cheeks with the damp cloth. He opened his eyes and frowned. His head was throbbing. As his vision sharpened, he saw Caitlin. She looked at him intensely, watching him as he became aware of his surroundings.

"Caitlin, what are you doing here? You must leave. It's not safe. Art might succeed in clearing the obstruction created by the explosion."

"Don't worry, Danny. A huge part of the tunnel has caved in and is still collapsing. We carried you to the entrance of the second tunnel."

"Where are the others?"

"They went on to find the cave with the water pool. They will come back later to carry you."

"No need. I'll walk."

"Hold on. We built a stretcher and tied you to it to carry you safely."

She unknotted the two aprons and helped him sit up.

"Ingenious," he said, realizing what they had done. "Now, please help me up. I'll see if I can stand and walk."

Caitlin supported him as he leaned against the rocky wall to stand up. He risked a few steps on his own. She watched him move, ready to intervene if necessary. From where she stood, he didn't seem secure on his feet.

"I was carrying a wooden box. Did you salvage it?" he asked.

"Yes, it's just here, outside the perimeter of the light."

"Ah, I see it now. Please look inside. I would prefer not to bend down. I'm still a bit dizzy. It should contain a powerful flashlight."

Caitlin gave him the flashlight, put her headlamp back on, and grabbed Danny's box. They walked slowly through the tunnel, Danny supporting himself lightly with his arm around her shoulders. He knew his way, and they didn't have to look for the marks at the tunnel intersections. They were engaged in the third tunnel when they saw a light approaching them quickly.

"Caitlin, Caitlin, we need you. Rihanna may be injured. She went into a tunnel to check out what was ahead and never returned. She's not answering our calls," Sarah shouted before reaching them.

"And none of you went to check what happened to her? You're all waiting for me to do it?"

"She's your friend," was Sarah's only explanation.

"Unbelievable! Danny, I'll go ahead and come back to help you later."

"Out of the question. I have explored all these tunnels, and there shouldn't have been any problems reaching the cave. Something went wrong, and running in the dark to save Rihanna can be more dangerous than helpful. You need me."

They reached the next intersection a few minutes later. The other girls were there, waiting, having retraced their steps back.

Danny immediately questioned them, "Which tunnel did you take?"

"This one. It quickly became too narrow, and Rihanna took it upon herself to explore it," Arianna said.

Caitlin looked at Arianna, seriously doubting the complete accuracy of her statement.

"That's not the right tunnel," Danny said, walking in front of the adjacent tunnel. "The tunnel you should have taken is marked here." Then, looking at the entrance of the wrong tunnel, he added, "This is dust, not a mark."

"Sarah, what have you done?" Arianna exclaimed. "We could have all been killed."

"Is that what you think happened to Rihanna?" Caitlin asked, her voice rising in anger.

"No time to argue," Danny promptly interrupted, afraid of an out-of-control escalation. "I don't know what Rihanna encountered. This tunnel was too narrow for me to explore."

CHAPTER 29

Operation Beth

December 13

ROBERT CALLED HIS team back to the room for a brief update. The atmosphere was tense, and everyone feared the worst after this unexpected summons barely fifteen minutes after the meeting adjourned.

Seeing them all standing up, anxious, he said, "It seems that events have picked up speed at The Enchanted Spring. Danny and the girls didn't have time to hide in the mountain as planned and might be trapped in an underground tunnel. We'll storm the facility today."

Then, he elaborated on a modified version of the plan before concluding, "Gear up; we'll be leaving in fifteen minutes."

Darkness had fallen when the three minivans, including one loaded with electronic surveillance equipment, reached the brick wall surrounding The Enchanted Spring. They stopped, and Johanna launched a drone at Robert's request to conduct a reconnaissance flight. She followed the drone's progress on the large screen of the minivan, with Robert and Ryan seated on either side of her.

A light snow was falling, and the deserted road leading to the facility was covered in a white blanket. At the entrance's iron gates, car tire tracks were seen exiting the facility and moving opposite their location.

"These are recent. I would say they were made less than ten minutes ago—they're barely covered by snow," Robert said.

"Agreed. We barely missed whoever was leaving," Ryan answered.

The drone flew over the gate and slowly headed for the house, following a stone-paved road. The road split in front of the house to encircle landscaping with an elegant statue of a beautiful, teenage girl pouring water from an urn she held over her shoulder.

"The Enchanted Spring legend," Ryan whispered, pointing at the statue.

Outdoor lamps lit up the surrounding ground, but the sizable two-story stone house, built in a traditional English manor style that looked out of place in Montana, was plunged into darkness.

"So far, there are no detectable mines or shooting devices," Johanna said.

"Circle the house. Let's see if there is any other incongruity," Robert ordered.

The back of the house was as dark as its facade. Johanna steered the drone toward an illuminated path wide enough for a single vehicle. The path led to a second smaller house and two utility buildings, then toward the mountain. The interiors of all the structures were dark.

"The path, like the road leading from the gate to the house, is not covered by snow. Heating elements must have been integrated into their structure. So, the electricity is not cut off, but nobody seems to be home," Ryan concluded.

"Let's confirm it. Johanna, can you activate the infrared and fly over the houses and other buildings again?" Robert asked.

Johanna conducted two reconnaissance flights over all the structures. No human or animal heat pattern could be detected anywhere.

"Boots on the ground," Robert said.

The three vehicles headed for the main road entrance. Johanna deactivated the gate lock using the drone's laser to destroy the control panel. Archie stepped out of one of the minivans to open the majestic iron gates. The minivans drove slowly toward the house and stopped in front of it.

"Robert, caution should be the rule; the house could be trapped," said Ryan, visibly nervous, vividly remembering Beth's ambush that had killed Pete and Officer Edward. "It would be wise to send a droid into the house first."

Robert looked at Ryan, analyzing his comment, wondering if Ryan was overreacting under emotional constraint, his previous experience clouding his judgment. On the other hand, rushing into the house would not necessarily result in anything good.

"You're right. Beth shouldn't be underestimated. Johanna, send a droid. Everyone stand by."

They watched as the droid climbed the few steps to the majestic arched porch and opened the large mahogany door without resistance.

"Wow, too easy. No one is home, and the door is unlocked. You might be right, Ryan," Robert said, concerned.

As the droid entered the house, the light turned on, activated by motion sensors. A sumptuous interior came into view. The entrance was guarded by two suits of medieval knight's armor standing with their swords and shields. The living room contained even more medieval mirabilia displayed on antique furniture and walls. A bucolic scene was painted on one of the walls, with tree branches reaching the ceiling and the sky and clouds completing the design up to the other walls. A hand-woven tapestry depicting a deer hunting scene hung on an adjacent wall. A large fireplace with an armory displayed above the mantel could be seen on the third wall.

They felt like they had been transported to another century for a moment. Then, returning to reality, Johanna led the droid back into the entrance hall. Opposite the living room was a room with a grand piano. The room decor was a reproduction of a French palace music room, with soft colors, delicate decorated faience on sophisticated side tables, and gold molding with vases and flowers plastered on the walls.

"To say the least, the owner of this place has eclectic taste spanning centuries," Johanna commented.

Further down the hall was a carved wooden door. It was closed.

"This is Beth's office and the premise control room. Danny mentioned that this room is automatically protected when no one is inside. Be careful," Robert said.

Johanna positioned the droid to the side of the door and directed it to open the door. As the door opened, beams of light scanned the doorway to locate the intruder.

"The droid won't be able to avoid the beams. Use Honeybee," said Robert.

Johanna opened a drawer in front of her, under the large screen, and took out a small box containing a miniature robot shaped like a bee. She then typed her instructions. They watched the small robot lift and fly away toward the house and Beth's office room. Honeybee easily dodged the beams of light and flew toward their source, a panel of electronics at the back of the room.

"From what I see, if these beams detect an intruder other than what they are programmed to authorize, laser beams will be fired from here," Johanna said, pointing to some devices.

As Honeybee flew around scanning the room, the shape of a human body appeared on the floor in the shadow of an imposing desk. Unfortunately, the light filtering from the hallway did not allow identification.

"Give me a minute," Johanna said.

Honeybee flew to the light control panel and landed on it. A moment later, commands appeared on the minivan's computer screen. Johanna hit a few keys, and the lights of the entire house flipped on.

Smiling, she said, "I don't like darkness."

Honeybee flew back behind the desk. They could now clearly see a woman's body, bathed in a pool of blood. She had been shot several times in the chest.

"That's Beth. Too bad, I wanted to spend some quality time with her," Ryan said, his fist clenched.

"Well, it's better like that. We both would have ended up in a lot of trouble," Robert said, putting his hand on Ryan's back and making clear that he would have turned a blind eye to whatever Ryan would have done.

Ryan nodded and mouthed "thank you" to his friend. Then, regaining his composure, he said, "I think it's safe to assume Beth did not anticipate our intervention before getting shot and didn't prepare any countermeasures."

"Danny mentioned a security system covering the perimeter at night," Robert commented.

"We still have a few hours ahead of us," Ryan said.

"Johanna, do your best to hack the system and deactivate it. If you haven't succeeded by this evening, we'll evacuate the perimeter for the night. Let's go inside the mountain," Robert ordered.

They cautiously proceeded through the mountain's entrance and down the main tunnel, stopping in front of the pulverized glass door of the hydroponic cave.

"Danny must have destroyed the control panel from the inside to prevent his attackers from easily entering the cave," Ryan observed. "This bought him some precious minutes."

"Let's split up and go through each row of crops. Be careful; some of the aggressors may still be here hiding," Robert ordered.

A few minutes later, the team regrouped in the small storage cave. Looking at the collapsed tunnel entrance, they silently assessed the situation.

"Whoever set this up overdid it," Lee, one of Robert's men specializing in explosives, commented.

"I don't think Danny had the luxury of time to estimate the proper charge," Ryan said. Then, pointing at the feet barely visible through the pile of rocks, he added, "He, nevertheless, managed to get rid of at least one of his pursuers."

"Whoever survived removed some of the rocks obstructing the entrance to clear a path inside the tunnel, but that only resulted in the collapse of other rocks. If we put things in perspective, Danny's goal was reached—the survivor gave up and left," Robert said, assessing the situation.

"Any chance we can clear the access?" Ryan asked.

"We'll need to shore up the ceiling and the walls as we progress. It will take a while to secure the passage," Lee replied.

"Estimated time?" Robert asked.

"Days."

"How about using one of your miniature insect robots to see what's behind it?" Ryan asked.

"I doubt it; it's too compact," Robert answered.

"We need some of our specialized equipment to find another entrance. Leila might also have telepathically received other information from Danny. I'm going back to the ranch to coordinate what is now a rescue mission," Ryan said.

"Good idea. We'll dig here meanwhile," Robert answered.

On his way back to the ranch, Ryan contacted Mark to inform him that Operation Beth had concluded with the discovery of Beth's body and told him about their new challenge in rescuing Danny and the abducted girls.

"We must work on other options in parallel," Ryan concluded.

"Agree. We'll fly in what you might need tonight. I'll coordinate Alex and Jack's flight from Alaska to Montana so they can pick up the equipment at the airport upon arrival and transport it to the ranch. Keep me posted on your plan and progress," Mark said.

CHAPTER 30

Rihanna's Rescue

December 13

THEY HAD REACHED the location in the tunnel, which had become so narrow that Danny couldn't go any further.

"This is where Rihanna ventured on," Arianna said.

"Caitlin, can you fit in there?" Danny asked.

"Yes, I can, sideways," she said, doing so for a few feet before retracing her steps.

Seeing an eager look on her face, Danny said, "Mark my words, Caitlin. You're doing an exploratory outing to find out what happened to Rihanna so we can plan a rescue afterward. Please do not, and I repeat, *do not* attempt anything on your own. We cannot have both of you in jeopardy."

He looked at her intensely until she nodded, and he gave her his powerful flashlight.

"Remember, always light up the ground ahead of you and proceed slowly," he said, squeezing her shoulder slightly to make sure she understood the gravity of the situation.

"I'll be careful, I promise." She then ventured into the tunnel. Barely twelve inches separated her from the rock wall. She soon disappeared from their sight.

"We can't see you anymore, Caitlin; tell us what's going on," Danny said.

"It's getting tighter and tighter; I can barely fit in now," Caitlin answered, discomfort tangible in her voice.

"Come back if you're not comfortable. We'll plan something else," Danny said, visibly worried that claustrophobia would make her lose control of her nerves. He preferred not to think about what would happen if she panicked.

"Caitlin?"

She didn't answer.

"Caitlin?" he yelled louder.

"I'm fine. I had to stop, close my eyes, and take a few deep breaths," she said. "I feel better now."

He sighed, partly relieved.

A few minutes later, they heard Caitlin's muffled exclamation.

As Danny was about to ask what was happening, they heard Caitlin talking but couldn't discern what she was saying.

"Caitlin, we can't understand what you're saying. What's going on?" Danny yelled.

The tunnel had sharply changed direction, and the walls were suddenly distant from each other by several feet. Caitlin pivoted on herself. She sighed in relief, the pounding in her ears stopped, and her pulse slowed. She could breathe normally without oppression. She felt liberated, free. She would finally be able to walk faster. She had barely walked a few feet when the light she projected in front of her encountered emptiness. She stopped abruptly, uttering an exclamation of surprise. A few more steps and she would have fallen into the abyss. She knelt and cautiously approached the edge of the ravine.

Illuminating the sheer drop, she saw a rock protruding from the wall about twenty feet below. And there, pressed against the wall, she saw Rihanna's body. Her eyes were closed. For a moment, Caitlin feared the worst. But under the intensity of the light, Rihanna opened her eyes and immediately covered them with her arm.

"Rihanna, can you hear me?"

"Caitlin, I'm so happy to hear your voice."

"Are you hurt?"

"I don't know. I'm stuck. I can't feel my legs anymore; they're numb. I'm afraid to move and fall farther down."

Caitlin projected the light toward the bottom. It was so far down that the light couldn't reach it. She brought the light back. Rihanna's lower legs were trapped in a crevice in the rock. It took Caitlin a moment to register how incredible the situation was. Rihanna could have bounced off the rock formation, fallen into the void beyond, and died. She shivered.

Moving the light around the surrounding walls, Caitlin couldn't see any easy path to Rihanna. She did not want to convey her disappointment and her assessment of Rihanna's dire situation back to her, so she addressed her with a cheerful voice.

"Rihanna, Danny has forbidden me to act on my own, so I'm going back to report to him. I'll make it fast. Everything will be fine. I'll get you out of there, no big deal."

"Don't worry; I'm not going anywhere. I'll be waiting for you."

Caitlin knew Rihanna well enough to realize her light tone was a mockery. She was aware of how precarious her situation was.

Danny questioned Caitlin in detail about the rock formation. He paused to think about a possible rescue plan before saying, "I have climbing gear, rope, and gloves in the cave with the water pool. Let's get them. But you won't be able to handle the rescue by yourself. I must get there."

"You cannot go into the tunnel without getting stuck halfway through. You're too thick," Caitlin answered.

"How about I join forces with Caitlin?" Arianna offered.

"Neither of you has experience in rappelling or climbing."

"So show us how," Caitlin said willingly.

Arianna followed Caitlin through the tunnel, helping her transport the equipment they had retrieved from the cave. Following Danny's instruction, they secured two steel eyebolts into the rock formation a short distance from the cliff and tied the ropes to them. Caitlin put on a harness. Once she secured herself to the ropes, she began her clumsy descent into the rock face, hanging only by her harness, until she reached Rihanna. Then, Arianna lowered a second harness.

"Caitlin," was the only word Rihanna could say before bursting into tears.

"I'm here; I'm here. Didn't I promise I wouldn't leave you here?" Caitlin said, reaching out to touch Rihanna's arm. "Please stop crying. We've got to work together to get you out."

"What should I do?" Rihanna asked bravely.

"First, help me secure the harness around your upper body. I'll then stand on the edge of the rock formation and kick it hard. Weakened by the crevice, this might cause it to collapse. Cling to the rock wall," Caitlin said.

Unfortunately, the rock formation was solid and extended far below the crevice, and Caitlin's efforts to destroy it failed.

"I'll have to break this rock. It'll just take longer," Caitlin said encouragingly. Then, looking up, she said, "Arianna, we'll need the heavy artillery."

A few minutes later, Arianna lowered a backpack dangling from a rope. It contained various tools, water bottles, fruits, and a basic aid kit. While Rihanna drank and ate, Caitlin retrieved a rock pick hammer, and sitting on the rock, she started shattering it in front of Rihanna's legs.

Looking at what she was doing, Rihanna commented, "Hum, this is what you meant by heavy artillery! I certainly do not want to discourage you, but we'll be quite old when you're done at that speed."

"Stop complaining; I'm sure you'll still be attractive enough for a poor guy to fall under your spell," Caitlin answered, working relentlessly.

As the tension around her lower legs was eased, the sensation returned to them and, with it, intense pain. Consequently, Rihanna was barely conscious when Caitlin shattered enough rock two hours later to free her.

Caitlin carefully pulled Rihanna's legs out and grew concerned by the extent of her injuries. Her ankles were broken, and deep lacerations were visible on her legs. She needed serious medical attention. But first, she and Arianna had to pull her up. She conveyed the information to Arianna.

"Wait. Rihanna is too heavy even for both of us. We need help. I'm going back to talk to Danny," Arianna said.

Caitlin began wrapping Rihanna's head and any exposed part of her body in bandages to prevent further laceration from the rock when she would be pulled up. After what seemed an eternity to Caitlin, Arianna returned. She lowered another rope.

"We're ready. Tie this rope to the harness—it's long enough for Danny to pull Rihanna. Shelby and Sarah are in the tunnel at different locations to relay any necessary information."

"Ready? Start pulling slowly," Caitlin said, standing on the rock formation beside Rihanna.

She heard Arianna yell, "Pull slowly."

There was a faint echo as the order was relayed. After a slight delay, the rope tightened, and Rihanna's body began to rise slowly. Rihanna moaned, vaguely aware of what was happening. However, after a few feet, her body hit the rock wall and started oscillating and bouncing off the rock.

"Stop pulling!" Caitlin said.

"Stop pulling," Arianna relayed.

"I'm climbing. I've got to stop her body oscillation, or you will injure her further," Caitlin said.

Caitlin climbed until she was equal to Rihanna's height. Ignoring any safety concerns, she used her body to absorb and stop Rihanna's body oscillation.

"Start pulling again," she told Arianna, who transmitted the order.

With Caitlin now at Rihanna's side, they start making good progress. Rihanna's body was only a few feet from the top when Shelby shouted, "The rope is breaking, the rope is breaking."

Caitlin climbed the last few feet and hauled herself off the cliff as Shelby stormed out of the tunnel. Both grabbed the rope behind Arianna. A few minutes later, the rope's frayed extremity flew out of the tunnel and fell to the ground. Rihanna's weight was brutally transferred entirely into their grip. The shock was intense, and they struggled as Rihanna's weight dragged them closer to the cliff.

"Hold on, pull!" Arianna yelled.

Sarah burst out of the tunnel and joined them in their effort. Their slippage stopped, and they slowly regained the lost ground. They finally brought Rihanna to the cliff's edge and pulled her over.

Exhausted, they sat silently on the ground for a moment. What sounded like a ferocious roar made them jump to their feet. They looked at each other, bewildered, before bursting into laughter after realizing it was Danny screaming his lungs out, his voice distorted by the tunnel. A second, even louder roar reverberated from the tunnel.

"Oh, goodness. All of you run back before Danny decides to come here and get stuck in the tunnel. We've done enough rescuing for one day," Caitlin said. "I'll stay with her."

To Caitlin's surprise, Arianna said, "I'm staying too. Let's take the bandages off and make her comfortable."

CHAPTER 31

An Early Morning Briefing

December 14

LEILA STEPPED INTO Robert's office at 5:45 the following morning. She was fifteen minutes early for the scheduled meeting but was nevertheless the last one to join. Alex welcomed her with an exuberant "Good morning, Sleeping Beauty" as he hugged her.

Before she could answer, Ryan cut in and said, "Good morning, Leila. We just started the meeting with Alex and Jack, who gave us the inventory of the equipment Mark sent us. Robert, what is the current state of work at the facility?"

"We are now in control of the property's security system. Johanna successfully hacked into it yesterday and disarmed it just before it could initiate its night surveillance mode. She's still working on the system controlling access to Beth's office. It's just a matter of minutes now before she succeeds. We'll recover Beth's body and confirm her identity. Her computer will probably be a useful source of information."

"How about the tunnel?" Ryan asked.

"My men worked overnight on clearing it up. Progress is slow.

The ceiling and walls must be consolidated at every step of the way. We stopped not long ago so my men could rest. We'll start over as soon as my backup team gets here. We'll work nonstop, in shifts, until we get full access."

"Leila, any new contact with Danny?" Ryan asked.

"Yes, I got in contact with him late last evening. He's desperate for help; the situation they are facing is dire," Leila told them about Rihanna's severe injuries, her need for medical attention, and the urgency of gaining access to the group. She concluded, "Danny had extensively mapped the tunnels and caves over the years. He had never located any other entrance, but since the air is not stagnant, and he had occasionally seen a few small animals in the tunnels and caves, we can assume that there are indeed other ways in."

"Any idea where we should start our search?" Jack asked.

"Danny estimates that the caves they are presently in are located on the other side of the mountain. We should start there," Leila said.

"Then, let's go on-site," Ryan said. "Leila, we need you on the rescue team," he concluded.

They stopped at the chalet occupied by Ryan's team to collect the equipment. Michael, Andrew, and Jason were outside, waiting near the already-loaded minivan. Shawn was farther back, facing the woods surrounding the chalet. As Leila exited the car, Shawn turned toward them with a large smile.

"Good morning, Leila. I have someone here that will be so happy to see you," he said.

Putting two fingers in his mouth, he emitted a long whistle. A few minutes passed, and out of the woods came Snow, jumping in the snow. Then, suddenly seeing Leila, she came straight to her, playfully jumping up. The impact made Leila lose her footing, and she fell into the bank of snow behind her, along with Snow, who was uncontrollably happy. Everyone laughed.

When Leila finally regained control of Snow, she said, "Snow, what are you doing here? I didn't think I would ever see you again. Look at you, all cleaned up and beautiful."

"I assumed she might be useful for the rescue," Alex said. "So, I asked the governor if we could borrow her for a while. I must say the staff at the dog shelter was more than happy to let her go. She disliked their company and was giving them a hard time."

Leila took Snow's head and said, "I won't let you go back there. I promised."

"Time to go, everyone, all hands on deck," Ryan said.

Leila looked at the boys. They were thrilled to be included in the rescue team.

Ryan told her as if reading her mind, "I can't leave them here alone. They're safer with us."

Leila nodded in agreement.

CHAPTER 32

A Crack in the Dark

December 14

RYAN DROVE TO the commercial entrance of The Enchanted Spring facility, which led directly to the mountain access. He punched the gate code Danny had given them and proceeded to where the facility's van was parked. One of the men Robert had left to secure the place gave Leila five bags, each containing a T-shirt from each of the girls and Danny that they'd found in the secondary house.

"Robert asked me to give you these, so the dog could pick up their scents," he said.

"Thank you," Leila said, putting them in the backpack Naomi had given her.

The mountain's entrance was a few feet away. Leila decided to go inside the mountain while the team unloaded and prepared the drones. There was a large platform with several empty crates. She pushed a few aside and sat between them. Suddenly, images from the water pool came to her mind. Danny was already awake. Two younger girls were resting nearby.

An eerie light was illuminating the cave when Sarah awoke. The mysterious atmosphere was conferred by the light emanating from the surface of the pool of water covering most of the cave. Looking around, she saw Danny standing still on the other side of the cave, near the cascading water, looking at the pale rays of light filtering through the rock formation. She got up to join him, trying not to wake Shelby, who was still asleep beside her. Danny was so absorbed in his thoughts that he did not hear her coming and jumped when she touched his arm.

"Sorry," she said. "I didn't mean to scare you." Then, pointing to the pool of water, she added, "This light is so spooky. I wouldn't be surprised to see ghosts rise from it and fly around us."

He smiled, taking her by the shoulder and pulling her closer to him.

"Don't worry, Shelby. I would fight them." Then, seriously, he said, "I have never been here so early in the morning, and I have never seen the pool lit up like this. There is a lake on this side of the mountain. This pool must be connected to the lake by a tunnel, and the rising sun must hit the tunnel entrance. The light is then reflected here."

"So, we can dive in and reach the lake," she said enthusiastically.

"We don't know the size of the opening nor the length of the tunnel. Moreover, the water is too cold at this time of the year, and we don't have protective diving gear."

"Will we be ever rescued?" she asked, her voice tinged with desperation.

He made her face him. Lifting her chin, he looked her straight in the eyes. She was visibly scared; tears were rolling down her cheeks. He replied with a simple but convincing "Yes." In reality, he was worried they might not all survive. He would blame himself for the rest of his life for what he had involuntarily done to them.

Spontaneously, she circled her arms around him and rested her head on his chest. Protectively, he closed his arms around her frail body. He hoped he had successfully transmitted the information on the cave to Leila. She was their lifeline, their only chance at survival.

When Leila emerged five minutes later, the team was ready to leave.

"Here you are," said Ryan as Leila joined them. "Found anything useful?"

"Yes, I can confirm that we must concentrate our search on the mountain's east side."

She explained the perception she had just received from Danny. Alex steered the drone to the mountain summit, and a few minutes later, it rose above the treetops. A lake came into view on the computer screen, illuminated by the first rays of the rising sun. The scenery was breathtaking.

"I can triangulate and find the likely location of the underwater tunnel entrance leading to the cave. Then, I'll extrapolate the outside location of the cave cascade," Alex said.

Less than ten minutes later, Alex entered coordinates in both drone computers of what could be the cave location.

"It's approximate, but the cave should be nearby."

"Alex, Leila, Jason, go ahead and bring the electronic devices with you. Michael and Shawn, please help me with what can be used for digging and drilling. Andrew, you're in charge of staying in touch with Leila's team and pointing us in the right direction."

Then, turning to Jack, Ryan said, "Prepare the diving equipment and get in contact with Robert. We'll need a boat. After we find the cave, we'll regroup and decide if we should dive."

Leaving Ryan and his team behind, Alex, Leila, and Jason started climbing the mountain toward the summit with an exuberant Snow running free ahead of them. Jason was monitoring the image transmitted by the drone Alex was controlling.

It took them about two hours to find a small water basin surrounded by a rocky formation. The probability that it was the location they were searching for was high, and Jason communicated their position to Andrew.

Leila took out the bags containing the T-shirts and opened a few of them. A characteristic odor of the underground cave and soil emanated from them. She let Snow sniff them. Snow started wandering around, her nose to the ground. It took her less than thirty minutes to find a crevasse that ran from the rock to the edge of the water basin, creating the small underground source. By then, Ryan and his team had joined them. They regrouped on the rocky platform where Snow stood, scratching the rock and moaning. A crevice was visible from up close.

"It's a small crack, but it's wide enough to slide the endoscope camera in," Ryan said, proceeding carefully.

A cave with a large pool of water appeared on the computer screen. In the cave's recess, they saw Danny, Shelby, and Sarah, oblivious to the camera's presence.

Ryan lowered down a miniature communication device.

"Good morning, everyone," he said. "May I have your attention?"

His voice produced the effect of a bomb. In a split second, they were all on their feet, the girls visibly scared, grabbing Danny's arms.

"The girls think you're a ghost," Leila said, taking the communication device from Ryan's hand.

"Don't be scared; we are members of the rescue team. You can see the communication device and the camera dangling from the cave ceiling in front of the cascade," Leila informed them.

Her announcement was greeted with visible relief. The girls released their grip, emitted piercing shouts of joy, and jumped up and down on the spot. Danny left the exuberant demonstration to come closer to the devices. They spent the next ten minutes updating their situation.

Meanwhile, Alex had kept busy figuring out how to break the rocks, enlarge the opening, and attempt a safe rescue. He signaled Ryan to join him.

"Solid rocks. Drilling manually or with a laser will take forever, and we can't risk a controlled explosion. It's too dangerous. The whole ceiling might collapse like in the tunnel. If not crushed by rocks, the dust will choke them. We should first investigate the diving option. If impossible, we can fall back on the drilling one," Alex informed him.

Ryan nodded, disappointed. Then, picking up his communication device, he said, "Jack, any update?"

"We have a boat, and the lake is not frozen."

CHAPTER 33

Underwater Exploration

December 14

"I'M IMPRESSED," SAID Jack. "Alex's calculations were quite accurate."

Ryan and Jack were on the boat, looking at the image transmitted by the underwater drone's sonar. The drone had found an opening in the rock where the cliff was plunging underwater.

"This could be the tunnel entrance leading to the cave pool. Let's have a closer look," Ryan said.

Slowly, Jack directed the drone inside the opening, gathering information on the tunnel dimension as it went on.

"It would be too tight for either of us to dive with our insulated suits and oxygen tanks," Jack said.

"You're right. We couldn't fit in even with a mini dive oxygen tank. This is one of the few times that I regret my strong build. The girls should be fine, but they will have to dive into the tunnel in a claustrophobic environment by themselves. Once engaged, there is no way back; they must go on. If they panic, they will die."

"Ah! The drone just reached the cave," Jack said.

"Bring it back. We must carefully plan how we are going

to proceed."

"I'll dive; I'll fit in there. The girls can follow me. They won't be alone in the tunnel; it will be less scary for them," Andrew said.

"Have you ever dived before?" Ryan asked.

"I did a lot of free dives in the pool with my friends when I was young. Moreover, at AgroFuture, Art's punishments consisted of confining us in a narrow, dark space, so I trained myself not to be afraid of it. It will serve me well here."

"Ryan, we're running out of options here. This solution must be considered seriously. The tunnel entrance from the storage cave will take days to clear and secure. Using the underwater access, Andrew can get the girls out, bring food, and antibiotics and painkillers to stabilize Rihanna's condition," Jack said.

The plan was for Andrew to follow the drone so its light would illuminate the passage. As Andrew was about to enter the tunnel, they saw sediments pushed out by the drone's propeller. Ryan signaled Andrew to wait and went on to peek inside the tunnel. He pulled out and shook his head, signaling a retreat to the boat.

"What happened?" Jack said as they surfaced.

"Sediments. The drone displaces them, and Andrew will swim in a murky soup, totally blind. It's worse than darkness since they reflect the light and create an illusion."

"If there are that many sediments, fins will generate the same issue when the girls follow Andrew."

"Yes. We need to minimize movement as much as possible;

otherwise, we'll need to wait hours between dives for the sediments to settle down."

They had devised a new plan: pulleys would be anchored inside the tunnel and at its two extremities, and a rope would be inserted into them. Using this system, they would transfer the girls' dive suits and mini oxygen tanks, and Jack and Ryan would pull the girls one at a time. Meanwhile, Andrew would ensure the proper march of the operation from the cave.

Andrew cautiously entered the underwater tunnel to install the pulleys and rope. The drone illuminated the tunnel from the pool, and Ryan and Jack were shooting the light of their underwater scooter from the lake. Most of the sediments had settled down, and to avoid lifting them again, Andrew pulled himself by grabbing the rocks on either side of him.

He had gone slightly more than halfway when he saw a rock shaped like a large stalagmite protruding from the tunnel's floor. He realized the rock would interfere with the pulleys/rope plan: if they brushed against it, they would risk tearing their suits. He had to lever it.

Ryan and Jack realized that Andrew had stopped; the rope tied around his waist was no longer moving. They wondered if he was caught on something. As the minutes passed, they grew anxious. Jack pulled on the rope lightly and waited. Andrew responded by pulling the rope once, indicating that everything was fine; Jack gave a thumbs up. Ryan nodded. Something was probably obstructing the tunnel, causing no issue for the drone, but too high or broad to allow a human to pass safely. Andrew was most likely removing it.

Ryan pointed at his watch. The mini oxygen tank was good for twenty minutes of easy diving without demanding high physical activity. They had calculated seven minutes to go through the tunnel, then about the same to secure the pulleys, leaving six minutes to spare. But if Andrew was removing an obstruction, he would use his oxygen much faster.

Andrew hit the rock again in a last effort, chipping it deeper. Using all his strength, he pushed it. It snapped. Knowing he was almost out of oxygen, he took a deep breath, drained his tank, and, using his hands, pulled himself firmly. It propelled him forward. He repeated the move several times. He was channeling his thoughts, forcing himself to remain calm: a few more feet and he would surface in the pool; he could see the drone, one last pull. He finally emerged from the tunnel and surfaced, having never been happier breathing freely. He heard the girls' screams of joy from the pool's shore.

CHAPTER 34

Underworld Portal

December 14

"I CAN'T CAPITULATE," LEILA said to Alex. "We must find an entrance giving us direct access to the cave where Rihanna is. She won't survive several days."

"I'm coming with you," Michael said.

They estimated the cave's location based on what Danny had told them, and they began a survey of the area with Snow. Coming upon a clearing, Snow suddenly stopped on guard, ears pointed and eyes focused. Looking in the same direction, they saw a motionless rabbit, hoping its presence would go unnoticed. But it was too late. Snow had detected it; she sprinted to catch it.

"We might have rabbit for dinner tonight," Michael joked.

The rabbit jumped a few times and suddenly disappeared. Reaching that location, Snow started digging. Soil was forcibly thrown behind her as she made her way through. Leila called her, but she didn't obey.

"What is she doing? She will get stuck in that hole," Leila said.

Then, like the rabbit, Snow disappeared. They approached the location to understand what was happening. Directing a flashlight into the hole, they realized, to their surprise, that it was not a burrow but a small tunnel opening into a larger tunnel.

"The portal to the underworld," Michael said dramatically.

Leila couldn't resist a smile. His fatalistic intonation reminded her of the movies and books about Hades, the frightening underworld of Greek mythology inhabited by the desolate souls of the dead. This boy had a flair for drama.

They enlarged the opening and went through. Leila called Snow. She barked back. They followed the tunnel in the direction of her barks. As they moved forward, they could hear a young feminine voice begging Snow to get help.

"It's Caitlin. I recognize her voice," Michael said.

He was about to sprint when Leila stopped him.

"Caution, Michael," she said. "There is a ravine somewhere ahead. If you run, you might not be able to stop in time. Your flashlight is not powerful enough to project light far ahead."

"Sorry. You're right."

They picked up their pace and reached the ravine a few minutes later. Snow was there, waiting for them. The ravine was at least sixty feet large. Caitlin was on the other side, Rihanna lying beside her, seemingly unconscious.

"Michael, is that you?" Caitlin asked.

"Yes. I promised to find you and set you free one day."

Tears started running down Caitlin's face—tears of relief at having been found and that Rihanna would be saved, tears of joy at seeing Michael again. Leila suspected Caitlin and Michael had bonded during Caitlin's "deprogramming" stay at AgroFuture.

"Caitlin, how is Rihanna?" Leila asked.

"She is drifting in and out of consciousness. She has several broken bones and must be hospitalized urgently."

Leila nodded. Using the communication device, she contacted Alex and Ryan.

"Alex, Ryan, do you receive me?" she asked.

"Leila, this is Alex. Ryan and Jack are diving. The rescue is underway. What's up? Your signal is weak."

"We found the cave entrance," she told him how to get where they were.

"I estimate it will take Ryan and Jack at least another two hours before they reach your location," Alex said. "I'll contact Robert to tell him what you just told me, and I'll join you."

"We'll build a suspension bridge," Robert announced. "Given Rihanna's condition, this will be the safest way to get her out."

"We will save time if we enroll Snow. The bridge would not need the higher guardrails required for a human to walk on it, and using a harness, Snow could pull a rescue stretcher retrofitted with small wheels," Leila proposed.

"Excellent idea," Robert agreed. "I will have the necessary materials to illuminate the cave brightly, build the bridge, and climb the walls brought here by helicopter."

The bridge was rudimentary—transversal wooden planks secured to two ropes crossing the ravine with longer wood planks screwed on their side, linking several planks and slightly stabilizing the bridge by creating a border wall a few inches tall. The purpose of such a border was to prevent the stretcher they would use to transport Rihanna from sliding overboard and falling over into the ravine.

Snow confidently walked on the bridge to cross to the other side as if she had walked on firm ground. The men involved in constructing the bridge from the other side firmly strapped

Rihanna into the stretcher. Snow started slowly crossing the bridge back, almost as if she understood her charge's fragility and their precarious situation. Halfway through, unfortunately, Rihanna became agitated. Her movements, even limited, resulted in the stretcher gaining momentum. It slid on one side, consequently causing the bridge to tilt.

"We need to compensate. Rick, Tom, quick, lie down on the opposite side of the tilt," Robert said to the men on both sides of the bridge.

The two men sprinted into action, stretching their full length on the bridge. The stretcher was now almost wholly leaning on the bridge's border, but the weight of the two men kept the bridge from tilting further. Snow struggled to pull the stretcher and to avoid being dragged to the side herself. She looked at Leila as if asking for forgiveness for being unable to fulfill the task she had been entrusted with.

"Pull, Snow. Pull. Don't give up, girl," Leila said, answering her silent plea.

"Come on, girl," Michael said, encouraging her.

And in a common spontaneous accord, everyone repeated Michael's encouragement. Snow reached into her strength and suddenly sprinted ahead, forcing the stretcher to get back in the center of the bridge and propelling it straight forward. Tom, lying on the near side of the bridge, barely had time to get out of her way. As Snow reached solid ground, Robert and Ryan grabbed the stretcher on either side to prevent it from rolling over on the uneven ground. Snow and her two helpers, running on each side, stopped a few inches from Leila, who took her in her arms as everyone yelled and applauded, overwhelmed with relief and joy.

CHAPTER 35

Final Rescue

December 14

As Rihanna was transported by helicopter to the nearest hospital, Caitlin, surrounded by Robert's men, climbed the wall. She had refused to use the bridge. Michael was impatiently waiting for her, and she took refuge in his arms when she touched the ground by his side.

They gave her a few minutes to recover, and then Ryan asked her, "Sorry to rush you, Caitlin, but could you tell us the tunnel configuration leading out of this cave on the other side? This exit might be the fastest way to get Danny out."

She nodded and gave them a detailed overview of the tunnel. Then, she and Michael decided to walk back to the facility, where a man would be waiting to drive them to the ranch. They left holding hands under the tender gaze of all. Without them realizing it, their sight was a balm to the hardship all had endured during this mission.

Ryan was the first to bring everyone back to the present moment.

"Back to reality, all; we are not done here. We need to enlarge the tunnel, but our rescue arsenal is presently limited for such a task unless we hammer our way inch by inch with a rock pick," Ryan said, designating the small pick Caitlin had used to free Rihanna.

"I'm surprised mining equipment isn't part of your arsenal," Robert teased. "Leave this one to me, pal."

He picked up his cell phone and speed-dialed one of his contacts. After the usual greetings, he said, "Pablo, I need a tunnel of solid rock to be slightly widened so a man can get through. Can you do such a job? . . . Now . . I'm sending a helicopter to pick you up. It'll be there in about twenty minutes. Thanks, see you soon."

"You want to metamorphose me into Spiderman?" Pablo asked, visibly uneasy as he contemplated the wall he would have to climb to cross over the ravine.

"Would you prefer to use the bridge?" Robert asked.

"Hell no. How can you call this aberration a bridge?"

Pablo's answer prompted Ryan to joke, "Robert, my friend, your engineering skills are really not appreciated at their true value!"

"Then, climbing it is," Robert said, ignoring Ryan's sarcasm. "You'll be fine between Ryan and me; these ropes will tie you to us. There is no danger of falling."

With apprehension, Pablo started climbing the wall following Robert's instructions. The contrast was shocking. Flanked by these two men, he looked tiny and delicate. Everyone was following his hesitant progress and encouraging him. He was white as a ghost when he finally reached the other side.

He lifted his index finger before saying, "Give me a minute to recuperate. I'm not used to such acrobatics. I'm comfortable with my feet on solid ground."

He sat on a rock and put his head between his legs. When he finally got up a few minutes later, his color had returned. He then went into the tunnel to estimate the work he would have to do and how to approach it. Ryan and Robert joined him and transmitted Caitlin's information.

"I think a mining laser will do the job," Pablo concluded.

They went back to the cave. Snow had transferred Pablo's equipment meanwhile using the bridge and Leila and the others had climbed the wall. As Pablo returned to the tunnel with his laser, he stopped anyone from following him.

"Sorry," he said. "I don't want anyone there while I work. It's dangerous. If the rocks overheat, they can explode. I suggest alternating our work: I cut the rock a few feet at a time, and you take my place and remove the debris while I rest. Then, I start over."

It took two hours to reach the point where the tunnel no longer needed widening. They were all exhausted. The rocks reverberated much heat, and dust filled the stagnant air. But the results were encouraging. The tunnel was large enough for a strong-built man to walk sideways without fear of getting stuck.

They all followed Caitlin's directives and reached the cave with the water pool in less than ten minutes. Danny had his back turned to them when they walked in and didn't see the light generated by their flashlights. He had lit a small folding camping stove and was warming up a can of food that was part of the survival package Ryan and Jack had sent him through the underwater tunnel.

Leila surprised him by saying, "Danny, you should join us for dinner. Naomi's meal is a far better alternative to this tin can."

"My god! You found a way in," he said, standing up and running toward them. "You didn't leave me here to die alone." He hugged Leila and started crying.

"Danny, that thought has never crossed our mind. We never intended to leave anyone behind," Ryan said, squeezing his shoulder.

"I'm sorry, I'm so sorry, but I feel so guilty. I deserve to die here. The girls... I should have questioned Beth and gotten to the bottom of this. Rihanna, is she alive? Will she survive?" Danny asked, choking with emotion.

"Don't worry; she's been rushed to the hospital. You'll see her soon since I think you should have your head injury checked out," Ryan said.

The children were all waiting for them at the main house. They were anxious to learn if Danny had been rescued and they questioned them until they related the rescue in detail.

"He's a good guy. He shouldn't be prosecuted. He did everything to save us," Caitlin said.

"I assume he won't. Your testimony should exonerate him of any wrongdoing in addition to other evidence we'll find on Beth's computer," Robert said.

The girls nodded in approval. Then, a heavy silence fell in the room, and they avoided making direct eye contact with any of them. Ryan looked at Leila, hoping she could explain what was going on.

"Michael, can you tell us what you all have in mind?" Robert asked.

"Well, while waiting for you, we discussed the trip to Alaska to meet our family. Don't get us wrong—the governor's offer is generous, but none of us wants to ever return to Alaska. We want to go home."

"The governor's offer is undoubtedly political. As soon as the news you've been found spreads, he will be in hot water. He wants to control the media to preserve his good reputation. But you will also be solicited for countless interviews. Journalists will be chasing you relentlessly. His offer gives you time to reconnect with your family privately," Robert said. "Then, there is also a matter of security; Art is still out there. We have to get to the bottom of this so you can live in security with your parents in Vermont."

"Ryan, Robert, can you ask your bosses to guide the governor's hideaway choice? Wouldn't an isolated island in the South Seas be a better place than any other places on the mainland?" Leila asked.

Leila didn't have to ask the children if such an idea pleased them. Their reaction spoke for itself: it was greeted with enthusiastic cheers, and all started talking simultaneously.

PART FOUR

CHAPTER 36

Family Reunion

Montana, December 15

THE GOVERNOR ACCEPTED the proposal presented to him with relief. He did not want to face the consequences of further attacks on Alaskan soil. It was concluded that a chartered plane would fly the parents to a private airport in Montana. From there, the children would join them to fly to a secluded resort in the Fiji Islands in the South Pacific, where they would spend the following weeks, including Christmas.

Naomi had suggested that the parents be reunited with their children at the ranch. So, a rented minibus picked them up at the airport and drove them to the main house. Rihanna's parents were brought to the hospital. She could not join the group on their journey, but the governor had extended his offer for her convalescence.

The parents were visibly euphoric as they stepped out of the minibus. They had set aside all worries about issues the children might suffer in the future to enjoy the present moment fully. Some parents had even brought what the children had cherished before being kidnapped, such as stuffed animals and dolls, to show them they had never been forgotten.

Shared or unique contradictory feelings were creating turmoil in the children's minds: the happiness of being reunited, the fear of not being loved for who they were now, the concern of what their future relationship would be and how to reenter society without being scrutinized at each step, the guilt of having been kidnapped, and the shame of having accepted their condition without further resistance.

Naomi and Sidney welcomed the parents as they entered the house, helping them with their winter clothes and introducing them to the living room. Suddenly, the children's anxiety vanished, replaced by tears of joy, kisses, and embraces. Leila, Ryan, Alex, Jack, and Robert watched the emotional reunion from a far corner of the living room. As the emotional intensity slightly receded, Ross, Michael's father, cleared his throat and addressed them.

"We all want to acknowledge our deep gratitude to the brave men and women who risked their lives to save our children. We are forever indebted to you."

Cheers and applause followed his statement, and the parents came to them to shake hands and hug them.

"Leila, you are my star," Ross said, hugging Leila. Saying so, he unbuttoned his sweater. He was wearing a dark indigo T-shirt with multiple stars imprinted on it. Right in the middle was a giant star with irradiating rays of light, and, in shining letters, *Leila* printed over it.

Leila burst out laughing but was deeply touched.

"I have a special announcement to make," Naomi said, interrupting all conversations. "Sidney and I would be honored if the children would come to spend some time at the ranch next summer. We promise some thrilling but safe adventures."

Cheers of joy welcomed the announcement.

CHAPTER 37

Unexpected Discovery

December 15

AFTER THE FAMILIES left, Ryan announced that he and his team would be leaving for Washington the next day, which prompted Naomi to ask, "Leila, why don't you stay? Christmas is coming, and unless you have other plans, we would enjoy your company for the coming weeks."

"Naomi, I'm tempted to say yes. This place is so beautiful. Having lost my parents, I usually spend the Christmas holiday with friends or alone."

"Be aware, my mother will make you work," Robert said, joining them and gently pulling his mother against him.

"Oh! Robert, don't be mean," she said, trying without success to extricate herself from his strong embrace. "To tell you the truth, Leila, I'll need your help convincing Danny to accept our offer. We intend to acquire The Enchanted Spring and want him to manage the facility. He might be reluctant to do so after what happened there."

"I think the girls might be your best allies. Knowing that they are thankful he saved their lives and that they do not blame him for their captivity will help him get rid of his guilt. After that, it will be easy. He is proud of The Enchanted Spring. He built it, and it serves a great purpose."

"I can help you robotize the place," Alex said. "We can model it on AgroFuture automated installation."

"Oh, that would be fantastic. I'm sure it will help him to consider our offer seriously," Naomi said.

The mention of AgroFuture triggered Leila's memory of the photo, and a nagging feeling associated with it resurfaced.

"Alex, did you ever have time to reconstruct the man's features in the photo you found at AgroFuture?" she asked.

"I let the program run in the background and haven't checked the result yet. We can have a look now if you want."

"I would love to. This man is probably Beth's father and probably has nothing to do with her criminal activities, but it's the only thing missing, and for a reason I cannot understand, I cannot let it go. It's not out of curiosity; my subconscious tells me it's important to identify him."

"You can use my office," Robert said. "I'll be giving Ryan and Jack a tour of the ranch meanwhile."

Alex typed a few keys and projected the reconstructed picture onto the office's large screen. The young man's extrapolated facial features appeared well-defined. Leila's face must have reflected surprise and puzzlement. Instinctively, she got closer to the screen.

Alex misinterpreted her reaction and said, "I'm sorry, Leila. Given what I had to start with, I don't think I can do better. Do you want me to run an age progression?"

Her eyes, wide open, were glued to the screen, her thoughts colliding at breakneck speed.

"Leila? Leila?" he said repetitively, wondering what was causing her fixation.

"Sorry, what did you say?" she answered without detaching her eyes from the screen.

"Would you like to see what this young man would look like now in his sixties or seventies?"

"Yes, please."

Over the following minutes, they saw the young man age in front of them.

"Oh my god," Alex said.

"There is more to it. You have never met Don Maharg, Alex. The young man's resemblance to Don in the original picture is striking—a resemblance that could only be found between a father and a son if photos of both, at the same age, were put side by side."

They stared at the screen, speechless. After a moment of reflection, Leila finally added, "Let's review all the facts from when I landed in Vermont five months ago based on what we now know. We'll need to do more research to nail this down. Then, when we have all the facts, we'll present them to the group. Operation Beth has just taken an unexpected twist; contrary to what we have assumed, it has not reached its conclusion yet."

"Let's work on it tonight," Alex replied. "We should be able to find most of it by tomorrow morning before leaving."

Over the night, Alex got all the necessary information to patch the holes as Leila reconstructed the chain of events. By sunrise, they had elucidated the entire case and had a solid story to tell the others at breakfast.

Alex concluded, "Leila, more than ever, I think your life is in danger."

Naomi had invited Ryan's team to the big house for one last

brunch before they left for Washington. Leila just had time to freshen up and change her clothes before joining them.

"What happened to you both?" Ryan said, addressing Alex and Leila. "You disappeared in Robert's office, and we haven't seen you until now. You look exhausted."

"We spent the night on the clothesline, as my grandmother would say," Leila answered.

"What?"

"We didn't sleep all night," Leila said, explaining the old expression. "We were working on the true behind-the-scenes story of the AgroFuture and The Enchanted Spring cases, clarifying Beth's and Don Maharg's roles, and most importantly, identifying the elusive mastermind, which has never been Beth."

"Please do tell," Robert said, vocalizing everyone else's thoughts.

Leila resumed what they had unearthed and the conclusion they had reached.

"Wow, I believe your deductions are straight on, but it will be hard to prove any of this," Robert said.

"You are not considering one powerful human factor: hatred," Leila said. "Not to undermine the important role all of you play in this affair, I was, however, instrumental in the downfall of each company that resulted in the deaths of Beth and Don. I was this killer's first target, and we must ensure I will be his last."

"How do you intend to make this happen?" Ryan asked.

"I'll contact Jordan Bergman, the Alaskan journalist, and give her a version of the story highlighting my role. It will further stir up his hatred and force him to act under its influence."

"We can't use you as bait," Ryan said.

"Like it or not, his quest for revenge won't stop until he kills me and then you. We destroyed his universe. He will not rest until it is done. We need to control the when and how."

CHAPTER 38

Settling Score

Houston, January 21, 2037

HIS HATRED FOR Leila was so intense that she felt his presence before he reached her house. He had been a master at hiding his thoughts before. She had never perceived his evil intentions, even in direct contact with him, and she had developed an affection for this charming, old, frail gentleman. But tonight, the gloves were off, and the intensity of his feelings filled her senses. She dismissed these impressions, not wanting to let him see the uneasiness they engendered in her.

She heard the back door being tested, the lock being picked, and the door cautiously being opened. He entered without making any noise and stepped into the living room, where she was waiting for him, alone, sitting in the half-light created by a low-intensity lamp. And there he was, dressed in black commando style, a gun in his hand, standing straight and strong, all signs of fragility gone.

"Good evening, Leila. I hope you don't mind; I let myself in. You need a better security system—the door was so easy to pick," he said in a soft, concerned voice, like a father advising his beloved child.

Again, Leila could only admire his control over his feelings and ease of conveying a false impression.

"Good evening, Willie. I was expecting you," she replied calmly.

"Ah! Your senses."

"Indeed. However, it wasn't my senses, but an old and damaged photo found at AgroFuture of a young couple immortalizing their love that helped me figure it out."

Willie's gaze grew piercing, and his facial features tensed, but he didn't answer.

She continued, "Alex smoothed out the imperfections and reconstituted the torn part of the photo. This allowed us to identify the couple as you and Gabriella, Beth's mother."

"Ah, Gabriella! We were so much in love. But her father forbade us to see each other. He claimed I wasn't good enough for her. She died giving birth to Beth because the old man refused to bring her to the hospital to avoid tarnishing the family's good reputation. Her death brought me to my knees. I left the village to join the army."

"Beth was your illegitimate daughter, the crowning of your love."

"Yes. However, it wasn't until after the old man died that I returned, told her I was her father, and gave her the photo you found."

"This photo also revealed a striking resemblance between you and Don Maharg when you were about the same age. At that point, I realized that his name, Maharg, became Graham, your name, when inverted. Then Alex discovered that Don Graham, your younger son, was once suspected of murder and had changed his name, creating a new identity still closely related to yours."

"Filial love."

"And you built a family business on filial love: Don oversaw AgroFuture and Beth ran The Enchanted Spring. However, I had difficulty understanding why you did not hire regular employees, especially for AgroFuture, where a limited number of humans was needed. Why risk it all by kidnapping children? Then it dawned on me: Beth's thirst for revenge gave you the idea of using enslaved children. Martha told me you taught history now and then at local schools. Your goal was to identify children with gentle characters. Then, it was just a matter of finding the right moment to kidnap them. This was your personal motivation: the thrill, the proof of your invincibility and your superiority over authority. Finally, an infinite portion might have been from a business perspective: no employee-related expense, a higher profit margin, no complaints, no strikes, total submission, and no disposal restraint."

"It's fascinating but not incriminating."

"Perhaps, but these facts forced me to reanalyze each event from a new angle. A little inquisition into your past revealed that you were once an elite sniper in the army. I was right when I perceived my attacker as a man at the hotel. It was you. I admit I still don't understand why; I didn't even know you then."

"I was a member of a special unit; I was aware of experiments using people like you. Some had great potential. With them, I learned how to project an image of myself, to bury my feelings to avoid raising doubts and inquisition in my thoughts. Anyone facing an enemy such as you must be proactive and take charge of the situation before it is too late. But, again, you have no legal proof, and Beth is still officially the number one suspect. Ballistics support it."

"Ralph's murder and the fire at the residence were other important clues. We had concluded that Nurse Brody was the prime suspect. However, while she was not praised for her compassion by the facility's residents, she was nevertheless not perceived as a murderer and an arsonist, capable of endangering the lives of several others to cover her crime."

"And you trusted the judgment of those old folks!"

"They made me realize that the facts could be interpreted differently. Alex discovered Nurse Brody had been previously convicted in another state for selling prescription drugs she had access to at her work. You were aware of her little commerce and asked Beth to schedule a pickup the evening of the fire to divert attention to her. Then, you scheduled the meeting in an open space where anyone could hear and oriented it so the conclusion was reached that Ralph knew the bunker emplacement and its owner."

"So, Leila, how do you interpret that night's events?"

"You gave Ralph a mortal drug dose and set up his apartment as you later did for yours, including a timer device on a delay. You then gave Nurse Brody and the janitor a concocted infusion spiked with sleeping pills. You mentally sent me a desperate SOS you knew I would pick up and come to your rescue. I should have been more suspicious when you seemed to find out that Nurse Brody was your assailant. If you had no suspicion of danger when you claimed she visited you, why send me an SOS? You then waited for us to arrive and drugged yourself a few minutes after our arrival. You were probably still conscious when Ryan walked into your apartment, and you triggered the device to start the fire. You never put yourself at risk."

"Why would I kill Ralph? He was a dear friend."

"A while ago, Ralph must have told you he was building the bunker; he might have even been your contact liaison with Gabriella then. He was a good man and would have come over even if it would have meant to implicate you."

"Your interpretation indeed, but I must say his death was merciful; he was sick, he had cancer, and he would have died sooner rather than later. May God have his soul."

His tone was so detached that Leila paused a minute to regroup before going on. On the evening of the vigil honoring the victims, residents and people of the village had praised Ralph as a man always ready to help others. They had quoted what he often said: "I am lucky to live the rest of my life among the people I love and who love me." Willie had killed his friend without hesitation or remorse.

"And there was this nagging question of why killing *you*, why inexplicably, were you the only one targeted?" she continued. "Ralph telling you the bunker's location? You would not have been the only one he would have confided in. To hide Stephan's drop location? He could have been dropped anywhere. In fact, you wanted Stephan to be found, so the quest for the bunker would end there, we would leave, and life would resume its normal course."

"Quite a story, quite an imagination," Willie said as if addressing a child.

"Willie, why play this game? We are alone; this conversation will stay between us since you intend to kill me. Do me one last favor. Tell me I have it right. You were the operation's mastermind, pulling the strings behind the scenes and sometimes getting down to business yourself."

"Don't you love mystery? The intrigue? Why indulge you? he said, mocking her. "But you still have unanswered questions. I will try my best to answer these truthfully."

"Did Sheriff Walters know about the bunker? Was it part of the plan to kill him?"

"No, but he knew the people around there well enough to conclude that the schizophrenic old man could only be the possible owner of such a place. So, he suggested Beth and himself spend some time at the old man's house celebrating their wedding anniversary, and when he thought Beth was gone hunting, he sneaked around and found the bunker, along with Nurse Brody's body. Beth had no choice but to kill him."

"Why did Nurse Brody take refuge in the old man's house, of all places?"

"Brody left because she guessed that her little commerce would be discovered. She never knew she was suspected of starting the fire to cover up a murder. Beth, as you suspected, was one of her clients. So, when Beth offered to hide her, she jumped at the opportunity. What Beth had in mind was to kill her so Brody would remain the prime and only suspect. Walters's inquisition messed up everything."

"You told Beth we planned to go to the old man's house. Didn't you?"

"Yes. But she took it upon herself to bug the basement with

explosives. The old man had everything she needed for that."

He stopped talking, openly smiling at her when he added. "Beth is also the only one who could have brought Stephan to the Enchanted Spring in the forest."

Leila was amazed to see how Willie constantly diverted all culpability toward his daughter, even implying that she might be the mastermind of the operation. And suddenly, it dawned on her: he utterly loved her; he was proud of her initiative, her Machiavellian mind and criminal actions, even more than he was of his son. Thinking of it, they might have underestimated her influence and her role in the affair after reopening the case. Beth had personally committed or been responsible for several murders and deaths. Leila even wondered now if the old man's death was natural and should be investigated. But a fact was sure, the apple hadn't fallen far from the tree: after all, Beth was the granddaughter of a schizophrenic and the daughter of a psychopath.

It was time to stop this madness, so she said, "Fair enough, Willie, let's say you are not implicated in your daughter's and son's criminal activities. The same can apply to me—I played no role in the deaths of Beth and Don. I didn't kill either of them."

In a split second, his smile was gone. Anger, reflected in his eyes, projected into his harsh voice.

"No, you didn't pull the trigger, but the chain of events you set in motion resulted in their deaths. Art killed them both. He was first on my list. I will grant you a quicker death than the slow torture I reserved for him," he replied.

"I don't think that will be possible. Your movements have been monitored since your return from Mexico two days ago, where you killed Art and his partner's wife," Leila said with a fake smile, then said in a firm tone, "Arrivederci, Willie."

As she said the password, a shot was fired from a shelf behind her. Willie was hit directly in the neck. He stumbled on the floor before even reacting. He was conscious as Leila leaned over him after pushing his gun away. He looked at her, trying unsuccessfully to talk. But it was pointless; she knew exactly what he was thinking.

"Alex has equipped my house with the best facial recognition system ever paired with a voice-activated protection system," she explained. "No, you won't die, but you'll be paralyzed for a few hours. Our conversation was recorded. Your role in my attempted murder, Ralph's murder, the kidnappings, and the exploitation of young children may be open to interpretation. But you just confessed to killing Art and breaking into my house to kill me. That should be enough to condemn you for the rest of your life."

The back door opened, and heavy footsteps hurried toward the living room. Robert and his men took delivery of their criminal.

CHAPTER 39

New Horizon

Washington, January 28, 2037

A WEEK LATER, LEILA was invited to Washington to meet Mark Landor. Ryan introduced her to his boss and then left. Mark indicated a sitting area in his office and immediately initiated the conversation as soon as she sat on the lovely, comfortable sofa.

"Ms. Rose, you have been an incredible asset in the Vermont kidnapping cases. They would not have been properly solved without you. I have thought about what I will say and consulted the team. We all agreed that I should offer you a job as a consultant. This may surprise you, and I suggest you take some time to think it over and contact me when you're ready. The job can be intense, emotionally draining, even dangerous at times, and you should seriously consider the implications it will have on your life if you accept it."

His offer took her aback. She thought of her parents, who had taught her the importance and the responsibility of using her gift for the good of others, of the feeling of fulfillment she had felt after Stephan and the other children had been found safe and sound and reunited with their families, and of the relief of putting Willie out for good. She thought of Pete, who had given his life for strangers he barely knew. Through the glass wall of Mark's office, she could see Ryan, Alex, and Jack, who had gathered outside and were hopefully expecting her consent. They had worked together, and together, they were a force to be reckoned with. She looked back at Mark. He seemed to be aware of her thoughts.

She smiled. "I don't need to think about it any longer. I've found my calling."

He got up with a broad smile, offering her his hand.

"Welcome to the team," he said.

As she was shaking his hand, the door was pushed open, and an exuberant Alex, followed by Ryan and Jack, burst into the office to give her a welcoming hug.

As Ryan hugged her, Leila felt a pang in her chest, and in the brief moment their eyes connected, she knew that there were far more than life-threatening adventures in her future.

AUTHOR'S NOTE

I loved reading but never thought I would write a novel someday. However, I guess it makes sense since, often at night, to relax and forget the day's stressful events and fall asleep, I do not take deep breaths or count sheep jumping over a fence; I tell myself a story. Usually, the stories are different each night and are forgotten the day after. However, a few years ago, Leila's story became quite consistent and kept me awake. So, I gave Leila her birthright by writing and publishing her story.

As I wrote *No Stones Left Unturned*, one song came back into my mind from my youth and imposed itself: "La Source," ("The Spring"), by the French singer Isabelle Aubret, the lyrics of Henri Dijan and Guy Bonnet, and the music of Daniel Faure. Readers can listen to it on YouTube and find a superposed English lyrics version as well. Isabelle Aubret sings in a soft and limpid voice the legend of a young and beautiful girl who is molested by three men and left to die on the moss in the forest. When the girl's lifeless body is lifted from the ground, a spring of pure water gushes out between the leaves and the stones. Sweetness, purity, and horror are reflected in Aubret's poignant interpretation. This song always affected me emotionally.

Climate change is on everyone's mind these days. To survive, we will have to develop alternative farming methods and drought-resistant crops. So, I felt justified to introduce the underground hydroponic culture in my story since it may become even essential in the future. It is already carried out in West Lafayette, Indiana, and Clapham, England. Underground caves and mines create an environment where a computer can tightly control temperature, humidity, light, airflow, and other plant-growth factors with minimal human intervention. Cultivation can be accomplished 365 days a year without being affected by the extreme climatic variations prevailing over each season and associated with climate change.

In our society, mind reading is associated with paranormal phenomena and science fiction. Mind reader synonyms are psychic, medium, telepath, mentalist, and clairvoyant, to name a few. More than anything, mind reading is considered an entertaining art, with performers using tricks, special effects, and psychological manipulation to "read" their audience's mind. Hollywood has also exploited the idea in film and television. Moreover, scientists deny the existence of phenomena such as extrasensory perception or telepathy. Physicists claim that telepathy, defined as the transmission of unfading signals across space, defies the laws of physics, and no specific region or change in the brain has ever been detected. So, Jeff and Ryan's strong opinion and denial of Leila's perception skill reflect the present consensus.

However, don't we all perform mind reading to a certain degree when interacting with others? Individuals with innate or acquired high emotional intelligence (EQ) pick up on subtle cues like facial expressions, body language, and tone of voice. This psychological concept is referred to as "mentalizing." Moreover, individuals, particularly women, with a keen sense of empathy and intuition can "read" people accurately. They connect with others deeply, put themselves in another's shoes, anticipate, understand, and share their feelings, and decode their emotions and thoughts.

No one can deny having heard or experienced a situation where someone dear, relative or friend, contacted you when you were thinking of them or of a funny or sad event implicating them. "I was just thinking of you," you might say. A powerful bond unites twins; they feel each other's emotions even before learning of the event impacting one of them. Children can sense their loved ones' emotions. Coincidences, skeptics would say. But can coincidence explain every situation?

Some individuals might have greater perception skills than others and may not be aware of them. We are not using our mental potential to the full extent. Our future evolution as a species might include developing our perception skills. Humanity might evolve toward a more empathic state before we destroy each other and our planet. Who knows what will then happen? Leila might then become more than a fictional character!

ACKNOWLEDGMENTS

I am grateful to my parents, grandparents, aunts, uncles, and extended family for their love and support. They provided me with a solid foundation. Whatever unfortunate events happen, I can securely return to the multiple happy memories that populated my wonderful childhood, lift myself, and move on. For those who have already departed, you live forever in my heart. I miss you all dearly.

My sincere thanks to Susan Steele, who was my first critic and left her mark in *No Stones Left Unturned*. Ryan proudly wears your name; to Anne Moreau for her judicious comments; to other friends and friends of friends who reassured me that this was a book worth publishing.

To the Köehler Books team: John, it has been a blessing for me to be accepted in your Emerging Author Program; Becky Hilliker, this book has reached a new level under your guidance and edits; Catherine Herold, your cover design is beyond anything I could ever imagine. Thank you.

www.ingramcontent.com/pod-product-compliance
Lightning Source LLC
LaVergne TN
LVHW041921070526
838199LV00051BA/2691